SHUFFLIN' OFF TO BUFFALO

"The saddlebags," the thief said curtly. "Hand 'em over."

Using his left hand and moving slowly so as not to spook Morgan, Longarm picked up the saddlebags. "Think these supplies will get you all the way to Buffalo, eh, Morgan?"

That surprised the outlaw. "How'd you know my name?" he demanded. "And how'd you know I was going to Buffalo?"

"That's where Donna is," Longarm said.

As soon as he hit Morgan with Donna's name and saw the desperado's eyes widen even more, Longarm flicked his wrist and sent the saddlebags spinning toward Morgan's face. At the same time, he flung himself to the side and grabbed for his gun.

The Colt seemed to leap into Longarm's hand as Morgan's pistol cracked spitefully. The bullet didn't come anywhere close to Longarm, who landed on his shoulder, rolled over, and triggered two fast shots while lying on his belly.

"Who . . . who the hell are you?" gasped Morgan.

"Custis Long, deputy U.S. marshal. And you picked the wrong pilgrim to rob."

DON'T MISS THESE
ALL-ACTION WESTERN SERIES
FROM THE BERKLEY PUBLISHING GROUP

THE GUNSMITH by J. R. Roberts
> Clint Adams was a legend among lawmen, outlaws, and ladies. They called him . . . the Gunsmith.

LONGARM by Tabor Evans
> The popular long-running series about Deputy U.S. Marshal Long—his life, his loves, his fight for justice.

SLOCUM by Jake Logan
> Today's longest-running action Western. John Slocum rides a deadly trail of hot blood and cold steel.

BUSHWHACKERS by B. J. Lanagan
> An action-packed series by the creators of Longarm! The rousing adventures of the most brutal gang of cutthroats ever assembled—Quantrill's Raiders.

DIAMONDBACK by Guy Brewer
> Dex Yancey is Diamondback, a Southern gentleman turned con man when his brother cheats him out of the family fortune. Ladies love him. Gamblers hate him. But nobody pulls one over on Dex . . .

WILDGUN by Jack Hanson
> Will Barlow's continuing search for his daughter, kidnapped by the Blackfeet Indians who slaughtered the rest of his family.

TABOR EVANS

LONGARM

ON A WITCH-HUNT

JOVE BOOKS, NEW YORK

LONGARM ON A WITCH-HUNT

A Jove Book / published by arrangement with
the author

PRINTING HISTORY
Jove edition / February 2002

Visit our website at
www.penguinputnam.com

ISBN: 0-515-13252-7

A JOVE BOOK®
Jove Books are published by The Berkley Publishing Group,
a division of Penguin Putnam Inc.,
375 Hudson Street, New York, New York 10014.
JOVE and the "J" design
are trademarks belonging to Penguin Putnam Inc.

PRINTED IN THE UNITED STATES OF AMERICA

10 9 8 7 6 5 4 3 2 1

1

Longarm got his first lead on the Bull Stennett gang in a little settlement called Buffalo, Wyoming.

He was bedding the town whore at the time, and as she thrust her hips up at him to match his downward strokes, she gasped, "You're the best I've had since Tom Morgan! Get that big ol' thing way up in me, cowboy!"

Longarm went stiff all over at the mention of Tom Morgan, and the whore must have thought he was coming. She clutched his buttocks and dug her fingernails into them as she pounded her heels against his back.

"Give it to me! Fill me up!" she cried.

Longarm hadn't told her he was a deputy United States marshal, and as talkative as she obviously was, he didn't want to. He didn't want her to know that he was interested in Tom Morgan, either.

So he drove his shaft into her a couple more times, and since he was almost ready anyway, he let himself tip over the edge and give in to his climax. Thick, scalding ropes of seed spurted out of his organ into her waiting grotto.

She let out a yelp or two and clutched at him even harder than before. Maybe when they'd started screwing she had only pretended to feel the passion she was exhibiting, but Longarm felt confident that this was the real thing now. The woman shuddered several times as she arched her back up off the bed. Then she blew out her breath in a long sigh and slumped underneath him. Her straight red hair spread out around her on the thin pillow.

"That was mighty good, cowboy," she said. "So good I wish I could let you have your dollar back."

"No need," Longarm told her. "You earned it."

And then some.

Tom Morgan had been riding with Bull Stennett's gang for six months or so, maybe longer than that. Stennett's band of owlhoots had showed up in Wyoming that far back, and there was no telling how long they had been together before that.

They had started robbing the stagecoaches that ran between Cheyenne and Sheridan, but the holdups had been strictly a problem for the local sheriffs and marshals until several pouches belonging to the U.S. Postal Service had been snatched. That made it a federal matter.

"Mail thieves, Billy?" Longarm had said to his boss, Chief Marshal Billy Vail, a few days earlier. They were in Vail's office in the federal building in Denver, and Vail was nervous about something. He kept taking his watch out of his pocket and looking at it.

Longarm went on. "You want me to go after a bunch of second rate mail thieves?"

"They're not second rate to the people they've killed in their robberies," snapped Vail as he checked the time again. "I imagine those folks thought it was pretty damned serious."

Longarm lit a cheroot, shook out the lucifer he'd used, and dropped the burned match on the floor next to the red leather chair he occupied. "Yeah, I expect you're right about that, Billy," he said solemnly. "I didn't mean to make light of any killings."

Vail pushed some documents across the desk toward Longarm. "It's all in these reports," he said. "You can read them on the train to Cheyenne and pick up a horse there. Henry has your vouchers ready."

Puffing nonchalantly on the cheroot, Longarm picked up the reports and began to slowly thumb through them. Vail's round, pudgy face started to get even more pink than usual.

"Better calm down a mite, Billy," Longarm advised in a leisurely drawl without looking up from the documents. "You'll have some sort o' spell if you keep getting all worked about whatever it is that's bothering you."

Vail finally lost his temper. "Just take the papers and go on!" he barked. "You've got your assignment, now carry it out!"

"Why, Billy," said Longarm, "it ain't like you to blow up like that."

Vail rolled his eyes and sighed ominously. Longarm was in the process of standing up when the door from the outer office opened and Henry, the chief marshal's pasty-faced clerk, stuck his nose in the room and said, "That journalist is here to see you, Marshal."

Longarm cocked an eyebrow at his boss. "Journalist?" he repeated.

Vail put his watch away, stood up, straightened his coat, and started rubbing his hand over the few strands of hair left on his bald pate. "I know you don't care much for newspaper folks, Custis," he said quickly. "I was just trying to spare you being bothered by some nosy reporter."

"Is that so?" murmured Longarm. Something was up here, and he wanted to find out what it was.

A few seconds later he found out as an attractive, bosomy brunette in her early thirties came sweeping into the office. Her dress was dark and sober, but it didn't hide the proud thrust of her breasts. The little hat perched on the mass of piled-up curls didn't conceal how thick and lustrous her hair was, either. She smiled at Longarm and came toward him, holding out her hand. She said, "Marshal Vail, I can't tell you what an honor it is to finally meet you! And I certainly can't thank you enough for granting me this interview."

Longarm chuckled as he took her hand and pressed it warmly. "Well, I've always liked having beautiful women feel grateful to me," he said, "but I'm afraid I've got something to tell you, ma'am."

"Oh?" She blinked big hazel eyes set under arching brows and flanked by cheeks dotted with tiny freckles. "What's that, Marshal Vail?"

"I ain't Billy Vail." Longarm let go of the woman's hand, took off his flat-crowned, snuff-brown Stetson, and gave her a half bow. "Deputy Marshal Custis Long, at your service, ma'am. This gent right over here behind the desk is Chief Marshal Vail."

"Oh," the woman said again, sounding disappointed. She barely looked at Vail, who, admittedly, wasn't nearly as imposing a figure as Longarm. Vail was a good administrator now, and he had been an even better lawman in the field in his younger days, but he wasn't tall, rangy, and broad shouldered, with ruggedly handsome features tanned the color of old saddle leather and a sweeping, dark-brown longhorn mustache. Longarm was the one who fit *that* description.

"Miss Parkin," Vail said, "I'm mighty pleased to meet you, and if you'll have a seat, I'll be glad to tell you everything you want to know about the U.S. marshals—"

"Parkin," interrupted Longarm. "Miss Esmerelda Parkin?"

"Why, yes," the lady reporter said, beaming at Longarm. "You've heard of me?"

"I've read your stories in the San Francisco paper when I was out there on a case."

"You've been to San Francisco, Marshal Long?"

"Sure, a whole heap of times. Why, one night on the Barbary Coast—no, wait a minute, I reckon that ain't a fit story to tell in mixed company after all."

4

Miss Esmerelda Parkin laughed. "Marshal, need I remind you that I'm in the journalism business? You won't find any blushing innocents in a newspaper office!" She put her hand on his arm. "Please, tell me all about your experiences on the Barbary Coast. I'd love to hear about them!"

"Miss Parkin," Vail said desperately, "what about our interview?"

"Oh, yes, Marshal Vail." She turned to him for a moment. "If it's all right with you, Marshal, I'll come back to speak with you at another time, whenever is convenient for you. I'll be here in Denver for several days gathering material for a new series of columns. Right now, though, I think I'd like to interview Marshal Long."

"But . . . but I've just given him an assignment—"

"All the more reason to speak to him now, before he has to leave, wouldn't you say?"

Longarm had been puffing on his cheroot and enjoying Vail's discomfiture. He took the cigar out of his mouth and said dryly, "The next train to Cheyenne don't leave until this evening, Billy. Won't take me long to pack, so I've got plenty of time to talk to Miss Parkin."

"But . . . but . . ." Vail didn't get any farther than that this time.

Miss Esmerelda Parkin linked arms with Longarm and said, "Come with me, Marshal. We'll go back to my hotel room and have a nice, long . . . interview."

"Yes, ma'am. The Justice Department likes for us to cooperate with the press whenever we can." Longarm grinned over his shoulder at Vail as they started out, then he paused and reached back with his free hand to snag the sheaf of papers detailing his latest assignment. He stuffed them in his coat pocket as he and Miss Esmerelda Parkin left the office.

He could feel Vail's eyes boring into his back as the chief marshal glared at him. Longarm knew he would pay for stealing this pretty reporter away from Vail—he'd likely get the dirtiest jobs Vail could come up with for the next month of Sundays—but he was betting it would be worth it. Miss Esmerelda Parkin was already making sure he could feel the softness of her right breast as it pressed insinuatingly against his left arm.

"Best close your mouth, Henry," Longarm told the gaping clerk as they went through the outer office. "You never know when there might be a fly buzzing around."

2

Miss Esmerelda Parkin had given him a fine send-off on his search for Bull Stennett, Tom Morgan, and the rest of the gang of stagecoach thieves plaguing the eastern half of Wyoming. What she had said about not being a blushing innocent was sure enough true, Longarm had discovered. She had just about worn him out trying to find out how many times he could climax in each of the various orifices she had offered to him. The four hours they had spent together in her hotel room had been plumb exhausting.

And he had nearly missed his train, to boot. He'd had to hurry so much to reach the depot in time that he hadn't had any supper. After running along the station platform, reaching for the grab iron, and swinging up onto the last car of the train, he'd had to make do with a stale roast beef sandwich and a mealy apple he bought from a kid vendor. He threw away about half the apple. Even one bite at a time it wasn't very good.

He dozed on the train, then found a room in a flophouse near the station when the train reached Cheyenne in the middle of the night. The next morning he rented a horse at a local livery and rode north on the ugly, hammer-headed lineback dun.

He had changed his brown tweed suit for denim jeans, a butternut shirt, and a sheepskin jacket that felt good in the chilly autumn air. The winds blew from the north, and it wouldn't be very many more weeks before the snows came.

Longarm hoped he had this case wrapped up before then. Wyoming could be damned brutal in the winter.

He'd meandered along from settlement to settlement, following the stage line route and listening everywhere he stopped for any news about the Stennett gang. Folks were still talking about some of the holdups, but no one seemed to have any idea where Stennett and the others holed up between jobs.

Until Buffalo and the redheaded whore with whom Longarm had indulged an impulse. She was young enough so that she wasn't used up yet, and she was sort of pretty in a rawboned way, and best of all, she knew Tom Morgan.

Of course, Longarm hadn't known anything about that when he decided to bed her. He'd been thinking about Miss Esmerelda Parkin, and he needed to ease the pressure in his balls.

As he rolled off her and sprawled on the bed next to her, he said, "Tom Morgan . . . seems to me I've heard that name somewhere before."

The whore reached down and fondled his softening organ. "You ain't the jealous type, are you, honey? You *do* know you ain't my first, don't you?" She laughed. "Hell, I doubt if you're number one thousand and one!"

He cupped the pale, freckled, pear-shaped breast closest to him and rubbed his thumb over the light-pink nipple. The nipple hardened into a tiny nub.

"I'm not jealous," he told her, "I'm just trying to remember where I heard of Tom Morgan before."

"Shoot, everybody in these parts has heard of Tom. He's a famous desperado. Rides with Bull Stennett."

8

Longarm shook his head. "Nope, doesn't sound familiar."

"Well, then, you ain't been around here very long, have you?" said the redhead, beginning to sound exasperated.

"Not too long," admitted Longarm. "I'm up from New Mexico, riding the chuck line and looking to see some new country."

"You picked a bad time of year for it. None of the ranches are hiring now. Won't be again until spring."

Longarm propped himself on an elbow and shrugged. "Reckon I'll have to find something else to do between now and then to pass the time." He lowered his head and began to suck on the nipple he had been toying with.

"Oh, yes," she breathed.

Longarm lifted his head a little. "Why don't you tell me about those outlaws? What'd you call 'em, the Stennett gang?"

"That . . . that's right. Bull Stennett heads up the gang, and Tom Morgan's his right-hand man."

Taking a cue from the redhead's words, Longarm slid his right hand down over the flat plane of her belly to the tangle of thick, dark-red hair between her legs.

"They been robbin' stagecoaches all over," continued the whore, "and all the lawmen in this part of Wyoming are lookin' for them. They lie low most of the time, but Tom, he can't stand to be away from me for very long. So he sneaks into town to be with me."

Longarm caressed the sopping-wet folds of her femininity, then slipped his middle finger into her while he rotated his thumb over the sensitive knob at the top of her slit. She gave a low, shaky cry.

"Sneaks into town from where?" he asked, then moved his head over to suck on the other nipple while he kept diddling her.

"I . . . I don't know for sure. Somewhere over west of here. I remember Tom saying something about . . . a little

9

valley in the mountains . . . hard to get to . . . not many people know it's there—"

Suddenly she began to writhe on the bed. Her hips bounced up and down frantically. Longarm stuck a second finger inside her and moved his thumb faster. She was drenched, and some of the moisture that flooded her had trickled down to thoroughly wet the puckered brown hole between the flattened cheeks of her rump. Longarm slipped his middle finger out of her gash and reached down to slide it up that narrower, tighter opening.

As he penetrated her in two places at once, the redhead yelped in ecstasy and flung her hips up off the bed. She shuddered and jerked for long seconds as her climax washed over her. Finally she collapsed in a quivering mass.

"I never . . . nobody ever . . . not even when one of the other girls played with it. . . ." Gasping for breath, she looked at Longarm and asked, "Are you sure you don't want your dollar back?"

"Nope," he told her with a grin. "In fact, I think I'm going to give you another one."

When Longarm left the redhead's room a little while later, he went downstairs in the saloon where the girl worked and walked over to the bar. The saloon wasn't a fancy place, but he had already discovered that the bartender had a bottle of Maryland rye stashed underneath the bar.

Longarm wasn't sure why a saloon in a wide place in the road like Buffalo stocked Tom Moore in addition to the usual panther piss and who-hit-John, but he wasn't going to look a gift horse in the ass, either, or whatever the old saying was. He put a coin on the hardwood and said to the bartender, "I'll have another shot of that rye, barkeep."

"Sure thing, mister." The bartender looked around nervously as he took the bottle from under the bar and splashed some of the whiskey into a glass. "Did you, uh, have a good time with Donna?"

So Donna was her name? Longarm hadn't asked. He felt a mite ashamed of himself for bedding a woman when he didn't even know her name . . . but only a mite.

"She was mighty fine," he told the bartender.

"Good, good." The bartender wiped sweat off his forehead.

Longarm frowned as he sipped the rye. A fire was burning in the cast-iron stove in the rear corner of the saloon, but it was still sort of chilly in the place.

So why was the bartender sweating?

"Will you be, uh, moving on tonight?" the bartender asked.

"Maybe," said Longarm. "I don't know yet."

He had the glass of rye in his left hand. Out of habit, he kept his right hand ready to reach for the Colt .45 holstered on his left hip in a cross-draw rig. His sheepskin jacket hung open so that he could reach the gun easily.

"I was just wondering," the bartender said quickly. "You said you were only passin' through. . . ."

"Might be I like it here," said Longarm. "I might just stay a while as long as that Donna gal is around."

The drink juggler's eyes widened. "Mister, you don't wanna—"

He stopped short as somebody stepped up to the bar beside Longarm.

The place was quiet now. There were only about a dozen customers in the saloon, and they had stopped talking. The shuffle of cards and the clink of poker chips had ceased, too.

Longarm looked over and saw a man with wide, bulky shoulders standing there. The stranger was dressed like a cattleman, and he was scowling at Longarm.

"Did I hear you say something about Donna?" he asked in an angry voice.

Longarm glanced at the bartender, who started to back

away. "Gave this gent the high sign, didn't you?" asked Longarm.

The bartender swallowed hard. "I . . . I had to—"

"Shut up, Pete," the stranger snapped. "This is between me and this son of a bitch now."

Longarm set his half-finished drink on the bar and said mildly, "I don't much cotton to being called names, old son."

"I don't give a heap o' buffalo shit what you cotton to, mister. What I want to know is if you been upstairs screwin' Donna!"

"The gal did seem to be for hire," Longarm pointed out. He suddenly wondered if this obnoxious stranger might be Tom Morgan. This man didn't really fit the description of Morgan contained in the reports Longarm had read, though.

The man jabbed himself in the chest with his left thumb. "She ain't for hire when *I'm* in town! Hell, everybody in these parts knows that."

"So they steer clear of her whenever you're around?"

"Damn right they do!"

"Only problem with that," said Longarm, "is that I'm not from around here. I didn't have no idea."

The man's rugged face looked slightly mollified. "Well, I reckon that's understandable," he said. "That's why I'm only goin' to beat the hell out of you instead of killin' you."

And with that, he launched a roundhouse punch at Longarm's head.

3

Longarm saw the punch coming and easily ducked under it. As the man's big, knobby fist sailed harmlessly over his head, Longarm stepped in and slammed a blow into his attacker's midsection.

The man's breath gusted out and he doubled over. Longarm stepped back, his right fist still cocked and his left hand held up, palm out.

"Hold on," Longarm said. "I ain't looking for trouble."

The man glared up at him. "You've found it," he rasped.

Then he launched himself in a dive at Longarm, tackling him around the waist and knocking him backward.

Both men came crashing down atop one of the tables where a poker game was in progress. Cards, chips, and money flew everywhere as the table collapsed under them. The players jumped out of the way, then darted back in to grab at the money scattered on the floor.

Meanwhile, Longarm was trying to defend himself. The stranger was lying on top of him, hooking punches into his belly. Luckily, their positions were so awkward that none of the blows had much power behind them.

Longarm grabbed the shoulders of the man's coat and

13

heaved as hard as he could. The man rolled off him, and Longarm went the other way.

The momentary respite gave Longarm the chance to surge to his feet. On the other side of the wrecked poker table, his opponent was getting up, too.

The man had a gun on his hip, but he hadn't made a move toward it. Clearly, he wanted to settle this dispute with fists, not lead.

That was all right with Longarm. He didn't want his search for the Stennett gang complicated by an unnecessary killing.

He didn't particularly want a brawl, either, but it was starting to look like he wouldn't be able to avoid that.

Still, one more try wouldn't hurt. He said, "Take it easy, mister. I didn't know you figured Donna was your girl. I'll even apologize if you want."

"Nobody humps that gal while I'm in town and gets away with it," the man growled at him. "Nobody!"

With a sigh of resignation, Longarm said, "We might as well get this over with, then."

With a howl of rage, the man came at him, swinging his fists in wild, looping punches.

Longarm fended off all the blows except one, but that one got through and landed solidly on his jaw, rocking him backward. He caught his balance, jabbed a straight left into the man's face that slowed down his rush, then threw a right cross that caught the man on the mouth. Blood spurted from the man's pulped lips.

The man stumbled back a step, crimson dribbling over his chin. "You busted my mouf!" he said thickly.

A savage grin tugged at Longarm's mouth. "Won't be quite as easy to kiss that redheaded gal for a while, will it?"

That infuriated the man even more. He charged Longarm again.

This time Longarm was ready for him. He straightened the man up with a punch, sunk a fist in his belly to double

14

him over again, and started an uppercut almost from the floor that sent the man flying back against the bar. The man hung there for a second, then plunged face first to the floor.

The bartender, who had watched the battle from a safe vantage point at the far end of the bar, let out a whistle of awe. "Damn, I never saw anybody do that to Tyrone Hardy before."

Well, at least he now knew the name of the man he had just knocked out, thought Longarm. Tonight seemed to be action first, then names.

Longarm's hat had come off when Hardy tackled him. He looked around for it now, picked it up, dusted it off, and put it on.

"That gent was spoiling for a fight," he said, looking at the bartender, "and you made sure he got one."

The bartender started sweating again. "There was nothing I could do about it, mister, I swear," he said. "Tyrone came in looking for Donna, and when he didn't see her, he asked me if she was upstairs with somebody."

"So you told him she was, and that when the fella came down you'd let him know."

The bartender paled before the angry, accusatory tone in Longarm's voice. "I had to," he whined. "Tyrone sort of runs things here in Buffalo."

"Important man, is he?"

"He owns the biggest ranch in the county and the general store here in town."

Longarm glanced at Hardy, who was still lying motionless in the sawdust that littered the saloon floor. "Don't look like much now," he commented.

"Tyrone!"

The voice came from the stairs. Longarm turned and saw the redheaded whore called Donna rushing down from the second floor. She ran straight to Hardy's crumpled form and dropped to her knees beside him.

"Did you do this?" she asked furiously as she looked up at Longarm.

"He started it," Longarm said.

"You bastard! I thought you were different. I thought you were nice!"

Longarm frowned. "But I tried to—"

"How could you hurt Tyrone?" Donna asked piteously.

There was a slightly calculated tone to her voice, though, Longarm realized. He was a stranger who would probably ride on and maybe never pass through Buffalo again, but Tyrone Hardy was somebody Donna depended on for a part—maybe a large part—of her living. When Hardy woke up, Donna wanted to be sure that he knew she was worried about *him*, not about the stranger who had knocked him out.

Longarm was willing to give her that much. He said, "He had it coming."

"You beast!"

She really wasn't that bad an actress, thought Longarm. But then, most whores had at least a little acting ability.

He could do a little acting of his own, he decided. He stepped closer to Donna, reached down, and took hold of her arm.

"Come with me," he growled.

For a second, real fear flared in her eyes. But he dropped one eyelid in a quick wink that no one else could see, and he felt the tense muscles in her arm relax.

"Leave me alone!" she cried.

Longarm hoped her histrionics didn't motivate one of the customers in the saloon to come to her defense. He didn't want to have to fight any more of Buffalo's citizens. He sure as hell didn't want any of them pulling a gun on him.

He tugged her to her feet and started toward the door of the saloon. The bartender called in a quavering voice, "Hey, mister, you can't—"

Donna turned her head and said, "It's all right, Pete. I'm not scared of this big bastard."

The bartender had a little gumption, thought Longarm. Had to give him credit for that. But he retreated quickly behind the bar when Donna gave him the opportunity.

Longarm marched her to the door and out onto the boardwalk, closing the door behind them. A cold wind was blowing, and Donna, who was wearing only a thin cotton dress, shivered as it touched her.

Longarm would have given her his jacket to wear, but he didn't plan on being out here with her for that long. He said, "Sorry about what happened in there. This won't get you in dutch with Hardy, will it?"

Donna laughed quietly. "Not hardly. Once he hears about how I carried on over him and lit into you, he'll be more in love with me than ever. He wants to marry me and take me away from all this, you know."

"Why don't you take him up on it?"

"Because I like screwing too much. God, I can't imagine what it would be like to only have one man ever poking me!"

Longarm grinned and shook his head. Donna grinned back at him and pushed her long red hair away from her face.

"How does Hardy feel about that fella Morgan?"

"Oh, he doesn't know about Tom. I have to meet him on the sly, on account of Tom's an outlaw, you know. Tom gets word to me when he's going to be in town." She frowned slightly. "Say, why are you so interested in Tom Morgan?"

"No particular reason."

Donna stiffened. "Damn it, you're a lawman, aren't you? Or a bounty hunter? I just thought of that." She punched a small, hard fist into Longarm's breastbone. "You just been pumpin' me for information, haven't you?"

She was really mad at him now, not acting. Longarm

didn't want her telling Morgan the next time he showed up in town that a big lawman with a longhorn mustache was looking for him.

Longarm took hold of her upper arms and pulled her against him. "You've got it all wrong, darlin'," he told her. "The only reason I pumped you was because it felt so damned good."

With that, he kissed her, and although Donna resisted at first, after a few seconds she seemed to melt in his arms. She sagged against him, molding her body to his as best she could with their clothes in the way, and opened her mouth to his questing tongue.

The kiss lasted a long time, and Longarm felt his shaft swelling and lengthening as Donna rubbed her groin against his. She took her mouth away from his and whispered, "Ever done it standing up in an alley?"

Longarm laughed quietly. "Sounds mighty appealing, but it's too damned cold for that." He glanced at the saloon window, which was fogged up inside. Several places had been wiped clean, though, and he figured some of the men inside were sneaking looks, trying to see what the stranger was doing to the redheaded whore he had dragged out of the saloon.

"Hardy'll be waking up pretty soon," he went on. "You'd better slap me and get on back inside."

"What?"

"Slap me," repeated Longarm. "It'll make the story better when those gents inside tell Hardy all about it."

"Yeah, I guess you're right." She sighed. "But I'm sorry."

"So am I."

Donna's hand flashed up and cracked across Longarm's face. "You bastard!" she cried, loud enough to be heard inside. She jerked away from him and whirled toward the door.

Longarm let her go, his cheek stinging from the slap. It was worth it, though, because he had distracted her from her curiosity about his questions concerning Tom Morgan.

It was a cold night and he didn't feel much like riding, but he went to the hitch rack and got his horse anyway. He'd worn out his welcome in Buffalo, but he had learned something in the process.

He swung up into the saddle and pointed the dun out of town. He would camp somewhere up in the hills, he decided, and in the morning he would head west.

Toward a little valley that was hard to find . . .

4

Wyoming was a big place. It wasn't going to be easy to find one little valley.

Longarm's only other alternative was to wait in Buffalo for Tom Morgan to show up, hope to spot him, and follow him back to the hideout. That would have been almost as much of a long shot, and besides, staying in Buffalo would have been complicated by the presence of Tyrone Hardy.

If Hardy ever saw him again, the jealous rancher would probably try to shoot him.

So Longarm rode on toward the Bighorn Mountains and Powder River Pass. He didn't know if the valley Bull Stennett was using for a hideout was on this side of the Bighorns or on the other side where the mountains sloped down to the Bighorn Basin. All of it was pretty rugged country.

Not many people were traveling this late in the fall. During the next week, Longarm encountered only a handful of riders, all of them cowboys for the various ranches spread out through the foothills of the Bighorns, and a couple of wagons carrying ranch families on their way to Buffalo to spend the winter in town. Longarm continued his pose as a drifting cowhand, and everyone he spoke to advised him to head back south to New Mexico Territory or Texas. No one was hiring up here.

Since he was pretending to be a stranger to Wyoming, he was able to ask questions about the country designed to bring out any knowledge of hidden valleys. Most of the cowboys were more than willing to talk, since theirs was a solitary existence, but none of them had any information to offer him.

Longarm was beginning to believe that Stennett's hide-out was on the other side of the mountains.

If that was the case, Tom Morgan wouldn't be able to get out to see Donna for very much longer. Snow was already falling at the higher elevations. In another week or two, all the passes would be blocked by drifts. It was time for Longarm to head for the Bighorn Basin, if he was going to get there at all.

Later, after he'd wrapped up this job, he could ride down across the Owl Creek Mountains, which were a lot smaller than the Bighorns, across the Shoshone Basin, and then skirt the Laramie Mountains all the way to the town named after them. The railroad ran through Laramie, so getting back to Denver from there would be simple.

Assuming, of course, that he lived through this assignment. If he was dead, all his travel plans would be pretty much moot.

That was what he was thinking with a grin on his face as he rode toward Powder River Pass. Mather Peak to the north and Hazelton Peak to the south both wore white caps of snow, as they did all year round.

The sky over the mountains was gray and threatening. Longarm wanted to get through the pass before nightfall, but late in the afternoon he decided he wasn't going to make it. He would have to look for a place to camp instead.

He was almost above the timberline, but he found a clump of pine trees that would make a suitable campsite. The temperature was still above freezing, so he was fairly comfortable once he'd built a small fire and set a pot of coffee to boiling. Later he would fry up some bacon and heat some of the biscuits he was carrying in his saddle-bags.

Darkness came quick and early this time of year, this high in the mountains. Longarm ate his supper as night fell and then lingered next to the fire sipping a second cup of coffee.

He had enough supplies to last a few more days. By then he would probably be close enough to the settlement of Greybull that he could ride over there and stock up again.

The sound of hoofbeats made him look up from his coffee. A horse was walking slowly toward the cluster of pine trees, coming toward the camp from the direction of the pass.

A moment later, a voice hailed, "Hello, the camp!" That was the usual procedure. Riding up to a camp unannounced was a good way for a man to get shot.

"Howdy!" Longarm called back. "Come on in if you're friendly!"

Just in case the stranger wasn't friendly, Longarm reached over and slid his Winchester out of the sheath attached to his saddle, which he had placed on a nearby rock when he took it off the dun.

With the clopping of the horse's hooves growing louder, the stranger rode out of the trees a few moments later. He reined his mount to a halt and asked, "All right to light and sit for a spell?"

"Sure," Longarm told him. "Got a little coffee left, and I can rustle up some more grub."

The man swung down from the back of the horse and patted the saddlebag on one side. "I've got provisions of my own, but I'll take that coffee if you don't want it."

"You're welcome to it," said Longarm. He sat on a fallen log with the Winchester cradled in his left arm. His right hand rested casually on the stock so that he could get his finger on the trigger in a hurry if need be. He was sure his visitor hadn't missed that.

The man was tall and well built in a denim jacket that wasn't really thick enough for this weather. His gray, curled-brim Stetson was shoved back on thick blond hair. A Remington revolver with ivory. grips rode in a holster on his right hip.

Longarm had known as soon as he got a good look at the man that he was familiar for some reason. It took the big lawman only a second to recall where he had read a description that this stranger matched perfectly. The ivory-handled revolver was the clincher. It had been used to gun down more than one innocent victim of a stagecoach holdup.

Longarm's visitor was Tom Morgan.

Grinning, the outlaw swung down from his saddle and stepped toward the fire. "Chilly tonight," he commented.

"Sure is," replied Longarm. His mind was working quickly as he tried to figure out how to play this chance encounter.

Of course, it wasn't as much of a coincidence as it might seem. Powder River Pass was the only way through the mountains in these parts, and anyone bound for Buffalo, Sheridan, or any of the other towns in northeast Wyoming would have to travel along this route.

Longarm had no doubt Tom Morgan was bound for Buffalo. Morgan was on his way to see Donna one last time before winter closed in.

One option was to let Morgan go on his way and then try to backtrack him to the hideout. That might be possible.

Another was to arrest him, take him back to Buffalo, and lock him up. There was no real law in Buffalo, though, and probably not even a jail. Certainly not one that would be likely to hold a salty hombre like Morgan.

The closest good-sized town was Sheridan. It would take a week or more to get there, then the same amount of time to get back here. By then, the pass would probably be closed by snow.

And keeping Morgan a prisoner for that long wouldn't be easy, either. The outlaw would always be looking for a chance to kill or escape from his captor.

"What about that coffee?" Morgan asked as he warmed his hands at the fire.

"Sure thing," replied Longarm. He leaned the Winchester on the log beside him and reached for his saddlebags with his left hand. He took out a battered tin cup and tossed it to Morgan. "Pot's on the fire. Help yourself."

Morgan hunkered down and poured the coffee, holding the handle of the small pot with a thick piece of leather cut and shaped for that purpose. He blew on the hot, black liquid, sipped from the cup, and nodded in satisfaction.

"Strong. Just the way I like it." He angled his head toward his horse, which stood with dangling reins. "I got a bottle in my saddlebag that would flavor this up just fine. You want some?"

Longarm nodded. "Sounds good." He hadn't figured out yet what to do about Morgan, but he didn't mind having a drink while he thought it over.

Morgan set his coffee cup aside, then stood up and went to his horse. He lifted the flap on one of the saddlebags and reached inside.

When his hand came out it was holding a gun instead of a bottle.

"Don't move, pard," he said as he turned and leveled the pistol at Longarm. The gun, Longarm noted, was only about half the size of the long-barreled, ivory-handled Remington. But it could kill a man just as dead.

"No need for that," Longarm said calmly. "I thought we were getting along fine."

"Sure," Morgan said with a grin, "but I'm afraid I don't have any supplies after all."

"You're welcome to share what I've got."

"I could go farther if I had 'em all," Morgan pointed

out. "And it's still two or three days' ride to where I'm headed."

That confirmed he was going to Buffalo, thought Longarm.

He sounded indignant as he said, "You can't leave me out here in the middle of nowhere with no supplies."

Morgan's grin widened. "Oh, it gets worse than that, pard. I'm going to leave you set a-foot, too."

"A man on foot can't make it out of these mountains!"

"Not with the wolves starting to get hungry he can't," Morgan agreed. "Now, I'll take whatever you've got, mister. That horse and your saddle and whatever's in your saddlebags. Hand 'em over."

Longarm thought about picking up the saddlebags and throwing them at Morgan in order to distract him. That wouldn't go far enough in evening the odds, he decided.

He needed something else.

Longarm wished he hadn't set his Winchester aside, but at the time he was trying to make sure that Morgan wasn't too suspicious of him. He'd been worrying about what sort of move to make, but Morgan had made *his* move first.

Once an thief, always a thief, Longarm supposed. Morgan hadn't been able to pass up the opportunity to rob somebody, even when, as far as he knew, it was just a pilgrim on the trail.

"The saddlebags," Morgan said curtly, losing his patience now. He repeated, "Hand 'em over, I said."

Using his left hand and moving slowly so as not to spook Morgan, Longarm picked up the saddlebags. "Think these supplies will get you all the way to Buffalo, eh, Morgan?"

That surprised the outlaw. "How'd you know my name?" he demanded. "How'd you know I was going to Buffalo?"

"That's where Donna is," Longarm said.

As soon as he hit Morgan with Donna's name and saw

the desperado's eyes widen even more, Longarm flicked his wrist and sent the saddlebags spinning toward Morgan's face. At the same time he flung himself to the side and grabbed for his gun.

The Colt seemed to leap into Longarm's hand as Morgan's pistol cracked spitefully. The bullet didn't come anywhere close to Longarm, who landed on his shoulder, rolled over, and triggered two fast shots while lying on his belly.

Both slugs ripped into Morgan's torso, one catching him in the chest while the other hit him low in the belly. He was knocked over backward by the impact of the bullets and dropped his gun as he fell.

Longarm scrambled up and covered the distance between himself and Morgan with a couple of big strides. He kicked Morgan's gun well out of reach, then bent down to snag the ivory-handled Remington and toss it away, too. Then he backed off, keeping his gun leveled at the outlaw.

"You're done for, old son," Longarm told him. Nobody survived being gut-shot like that. If Morgan was lucky, the bullet in his chest would kill him quickly. Otherwise the wait to die would a long, agonizing one.

"Who . . . who the hell are you?" gasped Morgan.

"Custis Long, deputy U.S. marshal. You picked the wrong pilgrim to rob."

"How did you . . . know my name?" Morgan coughed, and blood came from his mouth.

"I've been looking for you and Stennett and the rest of the bunch," Longarm answered him honestly. "You might as well tell me how to find that hideout of yours. I'm going to anyway."

Morgan ignored that. He said, "How do you . . . know Donna?"

"Met her in Buffalo. Seems like a nice girl for a whore. She's going to miss you, that's for sure. But she'll get

26

over it. Maybe now she'll go ahead and marry that fool Hardy."

"You . . . you bastard."

"What about it, Morgan? Where's the hideout?"

Morgan's lips drew back from his teeth in a grimace as a fresh wave of pain went through him. "Find it . . . yourself," he grated between clenched teeth. "And when you do . . . you'll be . . . cursed, too. . . ."

His head fell back as death claimed him. The unmistakable rattle of his last breath came from his throat.

Longarm frowned. What was that Morgan had said about being cursed if he found the hideout?

With a shake of his head, Longarm holstered his gun. He would have to figure out what Morgan had meant later. Right now, he had other things to do.

Like digging a grave.

5

Longarm didn't have any choice now except to try to backtrack Tom Morgan through the pass and back to the Stennett gang's hideout. Early the next morning, not long after dawn, he started, leading Morgan's horse. He had tossed the outlaw's saddle in a ravine.

Behind him he left the shallow grave in which Morgan's body lay, covered with rocks. It might not keep out the scavengers, but Longarm figured it was as much as a cold-blooded killer like Morgan deserved.

Donna would wonder why her dashing outlaw lover never came to see her anymore. She would probably figure he had come to a bad end and get over him, though.

Longarm couldn't help but think that she would be better off without him.

The sky was still gray this morning and the air was colder, but it wasn't snowing. Longarm reached the pass before noon and paused to twist around in the saddle and look back where he had come from.

The plains spread out to the east as far as a man could see. On a clear day, the Black Hills of Dakota Territory might be visible in the distance, but not today.

Longarm turned toward the west again. The mountains fell away in steep slopes in front of him, dropping to the

Bighorn Basin far below. This basin wasn't as big as the one to the east, so he could see the dark bulk of the Absarokas looming on the western horizon.

In between was beautiful country, prime thick-grassed ranching country where a couple of decades previously vast herds of buffalo had grazed and bands of Indians ranged free and proud and savage.

Now settlers had moved in, slowly but surely, bringing with them what passed for progress. Farther on, in the northwest corner of Wyoming, a huge area of land surrounding what was once known as Colter's Hell had even been designated a national park. Longarm had once had an assignment that had taken him to Yellowstone, several years earlier.

He wasn't one to dwell on the past. He started the dun moving along the trail, heading downslope toward the Bighorn Basin.

From time to time he saw some tracks that could have been made by Morgan, but it was difficult to tell for sure. First thing this morning, before breaking camp, he had checked the shoes on Morgan's horse for any telltale nicks or oddities, but he had found none.

Still, he was sure that Morgan had come from this direction. He kept his eyes open and rode on down toward the foothills.

It was late afternoon before he saw another human being. A couple of hours earlier, he had begun to see cattle grazing in the parks between stands of pine, so he wasn't surprised when he spotted a rider coming toward him. Where there were cows, there had to be cowboys.

Longarm reined in and waited for the stranger to come to him. The rider came trotting up a few minutes later. "Howdy," he greeted Longarm.

The puncher was young, not much into his twenties, Longarm judged. His face was open and friendly, and he had thick brown hair under a battered hat.

He wasn't a complete babe-in-the-woods, however. He

had a gunbelt strapped around his waist, and he held his mount's reins in his left hand while his right rested easily on his thigh, only inches away from the butt of the gun.

"Howdy," Longarm said with a pleasant nod of his own. "Mind telling me whose land I'm on?"

"This is the MK spread," the puncher replied. "Belongs to Martin Kincaid. I'm his son, Harley."

"Pleased to meet you, Harley," Longarm said. He wasn't surprised that the son of the ranch's owner was out checking on the stock. A lot of cattlemen believed in working as long and hard as the men who rode for them, and that extended to family as well.

Longarm went on, "My name's Custis Long." He hadn't been in this part of the country for quite a spell, so there was a good chance he wouldn't run into anyone who knew him. He decided not to use a false name, but he wasn't going to reveal that he was a lawman just yet.

"Pleased to meet you, Mr. Long," said Harley Kincaid. "You got business in these parts?"

"Passing through on my way to Montana," Longarm lied, "but I wouldn't mind staying a while, especially if I could find myself a job. Might rather sit out the winter here."

"Well, you'd have to talk to my pa about a job. He does all the hiring." The young man grinned. "But I reckon I can invite you back to the house for supper and a night's sleep under a roof. Pa wouldn't like it if I wasn't hospitable."

"Your pa sounds like a smart man," Longarm said.

Harley turned his mount to the north, and Longarm fell in alongside him, still leading the extra horse.

"I was just about to head for home anyway," Harley said as he rode. "It's gettin' dark earlier every day."

"Tends to do that this time of year," Longarm said with a grin.

"Yeah, I know. We'll be bringing the cattle down out of the hills into the basin over the next couple of weeks. Pa likes to leave them up here in the hills as long as he can, so the grass down below will last longer into the winter."

Harley was the talkative sort, Longarm decided after a few minutes of listening to the young man ramble. When Harley finally slowed down, Longarm commented, "Say, I heard a fella over on the other side of the Bighorns talking about a place he ran across on this side. Said it was a really pretty little valley, but it was hidden and almost impossible to find."

Harley's grin disappeared abruptly. "He must've been talking about Salem Valley."

"Could be," said Longarm casually, making sure he concealed his sudden interest. He hoped he had turned up another lead to Stennett and the rest of the outlaws.

"You don't want to go there," Harley said. "Nobody does, if they can avoid it."

"Why not?"

"Because it's cursed."

"Cursed?" Longarm repeated, remembering what Tom Morgan had said just before dying. Could there be some connection between the outlaw's odd words and what this young cowboy was saying?

"That's right," Harley said with a nod. "People who go in there have bad luck from then on." He paused and then added solemnly, "Some of 'em never even come out."

"Bad luck can happen anywhere," Longarm pointed out, "just like accidents."

Harley shook his head. "Not like this. A few weeks ago Joe Potter rode up in there looking for some steers that'd strayed off his place, and it wasn't but a day later that he got run over by a hay wagon. The brake slipped on the wagon."

"Been known to happen," said Longarm.

"Yeah, but the very next day? Besides, Joe was warned not to ride into Salem Valley."

"Warned by who?" Longarm asked. This Salem Valley

31

was beginning to sound more and more like a possible location for the Stennett gang's hideout.

"By the witch woman," Harley replied in hushed tones.

It was all Longarm could do not to rein in and stare at his new companion. Instead, he managed to keep riding along slowly as he asked, "Did you say witch woman?"

"That's what they call her. She has a place at the head of the valley, and she warns everybody who comes along not to go any farther."

"Is she some sort of Indian? Maybe there's a burial ground up in that valley."

"No, she's white," Harley declared. "As far as I know, the Indians never lived in Salem Valley unless it was a long time ago. But I guess if you come right down to it, I don't really know what's in the valley. My pa never would let me go up there."

"Sounds like an interesting place. Could be I'll go take a look at it."

"I wish you wouldn't, Mr. Long," Harley said seriously. "Seeing as I'm the one who told you about it, if anything happened to you I'd sort of blame myself for it."

"No need for that," Longarm assured him. "I'm a grown man. If I ride into Salem Valley it'll be my own choice."

And unless he came up with a better lead, he would be checking out the supposedly cursed valley, he decided. It was the most likely place he had come up with so far in his search for Bull Stennett and the rest of the outlaws.

A few minutes later, Longarm and Harley encountered several more cowboys who rode for Harley's father. They were on their way back to the headquarters of the MK ranch, too.

Harley introduced Longarm to the other men and added, "Mr. Long's looking for a job."

One of the men, a beefy fellow who'd been introduced to Longarm as Jed Ashcroft, grunted and said, "Grub-line rider, are you?"

"You could say that," Longarm replied.

Ashcroft gnawed on his thick mustache, then said, "Well, I'm sorry, Long, but I expect Mr. Kincaid will tell you he ain't hirin'. I'm ramrod on the MK, and I know we got a full crew."

Longarm shrugged. "Don't reckon it'd hurt to ask."

"No, and you're welcome to a hot meal and a bunk for the night, either way."

They rode on and a half hour later came to a small hill situated in a broad valley. The ranch house, a large log structure with an impressive porch on the front of it, sat atop the hill with a few pine trees around it. The barns, corrals, bunkhouse, blacksmith shop, and smokehouse were located at the base of the hill.

"That's the MK," Harley said.

"Nice place," Longarm said. "How long has it been since your pa settled here?"

"Fifteen years. I was only six when he brought me and my ma out here. I was helping to fight Indians when I was eight," Harley added proudly.

"Then the MK must've been one of the first spreads in these parts."

"That's right." Harley frowned slightly. "Say, I thought you were a stranger around here. How do you know when the area was first settled?"

Longarm shrugged. "A fella hears talk. I like to listen."

"Oh." Harley nodded, accepting Longarm's answer.

The group rode up to the biggest barn and dismounted. Jed Ashcroft offered, "I'll take care of that dun for you, Long," and took the reins from Longarm.

"Much obliged," Longarm told the ranch foreman. He and Harley walked past a buggy that was parked by the barn and headed up the hill toward the house.

Harley had just put a foot on the bottom step leading up to the porch when inside the house someone yelled, "Son of a bitch!" Hard on the heels of the shout, Longarm heard the ugly thud of a fist landing on flesh.

An instant later, a man came sailing through the open front door to land on his back with a resounding crash.

33

6

Harley let out an alarmed yell and practically leaped to the porch. "Nick!" he said. "Nick, are you all right?"

The man lying on the porch sat up shakily and rubbed his jaw as Harley knelt next to him. "Yeah, I'm all right," he said. "Your pa just clouted me one, that's all."

He was several years older than Harley, with brown hair that kept trying to fall down over his eyes. He wore a gray tweed suit, and a glance at his soft hands told Longarm he was no cowboy.

Another man strode out onto the porch and glared down at Nick. "You still here?" he demanded.

"I haven't had time to get up since you knocked me down," Nick said. He added caustically, "Sorry."

The newcomer was a middle-aged man of medium height, stocky and broad shouldered. His blond hair was shot through with gray, as was the mustache that drooped over his wide mouth.

"A fella who comes into my house and tells me my land ain't really my land ought to expect to get knocked down," he snapped.

"Blast it, Pa," Harley said, "Nick's our friend!"

"He's a lawyer," Martin Kincaid said with a dismissive flip of his hand.

Nick got to his feet with Harley's help and straightened his coat. "You may not want to believe it, Mr. Kincaid, but I'm trying to help you," he said.

Kincaid snorted contemptuously. "Help me right off my land is what you mean."

"No, sir. I want you to file a proper claim to your ranch, as the government now requires, so that you *won't* lose it."

"You mean I have to ride all the way to Greybull and sign my name on some damn piece of paper to prove that the land I've held for fifteen years is really mine?" Kincaid pointed a finger toward a small plot of ground surrounded by a wooden fence and several pine trees. "The land where my wife is buried?"

Harley began saying, "Pa, if that's what the law is now—"

"To hell with the law!" Kincaid broke in. "I've done all the talkin' I'm goin' to do." He turned and stomped into the house, slamming the door behind him.

"I'm sorry, Nick," Harley said, turning to the other young man. He made a helpless gesture toward the door. "You know how he is."

"Yes, but he doesn't know how other people are. Someone's going to steal this place out from under him if he won't listen to reason, Harley." Nick glanced over at Longarm, who had watched the exchange with only casual interest, since it didn't have anything to do with the job that had brought him up here. "Who's this?"

"Oh, yeah," Harley said. "Nick Larson, this is Custis Long. Mr. Long, Nick Larson from the county seat over at Greybull."

Longarm shook hands with Nick Larson. "Pleased to meet you," he said, although a lot of the time he pretty much shared Martin Kincaid's low opinion of lawyers.

"What brings you to the MK, Mr. Long?" asked Larson.

"Looking for work."

Larson shook his head. "I doubt you'll find it here, given the time of year that it is."

Larson might not be a cattleman, but clearly he knew something about the business. Practicing law as he did in Greybull, he probably represented many of the ranchers in the Bighorn Basin.

"Well, if nothing else I've gotten to see some pretty country," said Longarm.

"That's true. You won't find much prettier." Larson turned to Harley. "I left my hat in there. . . ."

"I'll get it for you," Harley quickly offered. "Mr. Long, come on inside and I'll introduce you to Pa."

Longarm followed Harley into the house, leaving Nick Larson on the porch. Harley picked up a gray hat from a small table just inside the door and handed it back out to Larson.

"Try to talk some sense into his head," Larson said quietly, then lifted a hand in farewell as he started down the hill. Longarm figured the buggy he had noticed parked beside the barn belonged to the attorney.

The front room of the ranch house was big and sprawling, with a massive fireplace on the far wall, heavy furniture, and woven rugs on the floor. Martin Kincaid stood near the fireplace, a glass in his hand.

He lifted the glass and tossed off the liquor in it, then turned toward his son. "Who's this?" he asked bluntly as he jabbed a thumb toward Longarm.

"This is Custis Long, Pa. I met him up in the hills while I was checking the stock."

Longarm extended his hand. "Pleased to meet you, Mr. Kincaid."

Kincaid's grip was firm and strong. "You don't look like a regular drifter."

"Thanks," Longarm said with a chuckle. "I reckon that's what I am, though. Looking for work."

Kincaid shook his head. "Sorry, not here. I've got all the hands I need until spring roundup."

"That's what folks keep telling me. Your boy here, though, said I was welcome to stay for supper whether you had a job for me or not."

"Damn right. I never yet turned a man away from my table. My wife wouldn't have heard of being inhospitable while she was alive, and neither will I."

That was common practice throughout the West, Longarm knew. With a few notable exceptions, frontier folks were some of the friendliest in the world.

"Supper'll be ready in a while," Kincaid went on. "Until then, how about a drink?"

Longarm grinned. "Sounds good to me."

Kincaid went to a sideboard and got a bottle and glass. He poured a drink and handed it to Longarm, who sipped the whiskey and then licked his lips appreciatively.

"Pa," said Harley, "I think you ought to listen to what Nick has to say. He's just trying to help."

Stubbornly, Kincaid shook his head. "I don't need no lawyer helpin' me hold land that's already mine."

"It may not be yours much longer unless you file a proper claim," Harley insisted. "Nick says somebody could steal the MK out from under you."

"Somebody," Kincaid repeated with a snort. "What you mean is that Crawford woman."

"Beth Crawford doesn't want this ranch, Pa. She and her niece already have as much land as they can handle, just the two of them and that old man."

Kincaid scowled and poured himself another drink. "Everybody wants to grow," he insisted. "The Crawford spread can't extend into Salem Valley, so it's got to come this way, toward our range."

Longarm's ears perked up. He said, "This here Salem Valley is the place you were telling me about earlier, ain't it, Harley?"

The young man nodded. "That's right. The MK range runs almost up to the entrance to the valley, but Miz Crawford and her niece homesteaded on the little piece of ground that was in between. They run a few cattle on it, but their spread doesn't amount to much."

Longarm cast his mind back over everything Harley had told him earlier. "Then this Crawford woman you're talking about, she'd be—"

"The witch," Harley finished for him. "That's right."

Martin Kincaid snorted again. "Witch," he repeated. "You got the wrong letter startin' out that word, boy."

"You don't believe in witches, Mr. Kincaid?" asked Longarm.

"I'm hardheaded enough so that I don't believe in much of anything I can't see," declared Kincaid.

Harley said, "What about the curse on Salem Valley?"

"The only curse on that valley is that uppity woman sittin' smack-dab in the entrance and warnin' everybody off!"

That was all mighty interesting, thought Longarm. Beth Crawford tried to keep folks away from Salem Valley by telling them it was cursed. Tom Morgan had said with his dying breath that if Longarm found the valley the Stennett gang was using for a hideout, then he would be cursed.

That couldn't be a coincidence, Longarm decided. There had to be a connection between Stennett and Beth Crawford. Maybe she kept people away from the hideout and spread stories about curses in return for a share of the loot from the gang's holdups.

Longarm could tell right now that he was going to have to pay a visit to Salem Valley—and Beth Crawford.

Harley Kincaid turned to Longarm. "Sorry to bore you with our problems, Mr. Long. I reckon supper'll be ready soon."

His father nodded. "That's right. I'll go out to the cook shack and see what's keeping Horse Collar."

Kincaid tossed back the rest of his drink, set the empty glass on the sideboard, and stalked out of the room. Longarm looked at Harley and asked, "Did he say Horse Collar?"

"That's our cook, Horse Collar Jones. Best ranch cook in all of Wyoming. He drove the chuck wagon when Pa brought his first herd out here."

Longarm nodded. He was sure there was a good reason for the cook's colorful nickname. Probably he would find it out later.

In the meantime, he had to get directions to Salem Valley, because as soon as it was possible, probably the next day, he intended to have a look at the cursed valley for himself.

7

Longarm decided that Horse Collar Jones had gotten his name from the way he looked: his long face and prominent ears made him slightly resemble a horse collar if you looked at him the right way.

One thing that wasn't in doubt was the old man's ability in the cook shack. The stew he served for supper was as good as Longarm had tasted lately, and the deep-dish apple pie was even better.

The ranch hands ate in the house with the Kincaids, and afterward Longarm went back to the bunkhouse with them. As a supposed grub-line rider, that was the natural thing for him to do.

He sat in on a poker game played for matchsticks and shared his cheroots with the other players. Through a blue haze of smoke, Longarm made conversation that seemed idle but was actually anything but.

"That lawyer fella from Greybull sure is anxious for Kincaid to file a proper claim on the ranch," he commented as he studied his cards.

"I reckon that's the boss's business," said Jed Ashcroft. "I figger he'll do whatever's best."

"I'm sure he will. Me, I don't like having anything to do with lawyers."

One of the other punchers said, "Aw, Larson's all right for a dude. He was at that fancy college back East where the old man sent Harley for some schoolin'."

"Harley went to college?" Longarm asked.

"Yep," Ashcroft said with a nod. "Only it didn't take. He just wanted to come back out here and ride the range with the rest of us, like he'd always done. The boss finally gave in. When Harley got off the stage in Greybull, Nick Larson was with him. He come west to start his practice after makin' friends with Harley."

Longarm discarded, took two more, and didn't like them any better so he folded when the betting came around to him. He puffed on his cheroot for a minute, then said, "What's all this about some valley that's supposed to be cursed?"

"It *is* cursed," one of the cowboys said without hesitation. "I tell you, you couldn't pay me enough to ride up in there, no matter how many strays there are that've wandered up there."

"I've heard of places having an Indian curse on them," Longarm began.

"This ain't no Injun curse," the puncher said. "It was that witch woman who done it."

"Beth Crawford?"

"That's her name," Ashcroft said heavily. "What business is it of yours, Long?"

Longarm shook his head. "None at all. Just making conversation, that's all."

Ashcroft said, "Ah, hell, I fold," and tossed his cards on the pile. He looked at Longarm and went on, "I don't even like to have folks talkin' about such things around here. Makes me nervous."

Longarm wouldn't have thought that anything would make a salty old rannihan like Ashcroft nervous. He pushed the issue by saying, "Harley said some folks who've ridden into Salem Valley never came back."

One of the other punchers leaned forward. "That's

41

right. Morg Holmes, an hombre who used to ride for the REH Connected, rode up there, and none of us ever saw him again."

Ashcroft snapped, "I heard tell he went back East where he came from."

"Nobody saw him go if he did. And what about that lanky redheaded fella called Burke? He disappeared, too."

The rest of the men started throwing in other names, all of them punchers who had supposedly vanished in Salem Valley.

Longarm had an idea what had happened to them. They had probably run into the Stennett gang and been killed, and now their bodies were either in shallow graves or dumped in the bottom of a ravine somewhere.

After a few minutes, Jed Ashcroft slapped a palm down on the table, making the matchsticks in the center jump. "Damn it, I said I didn't want a bunch of talk like this! You fellers'll sit around and scare yourselves silly, and first thing you know you'll be jumpin' at your own shadows!"

"Sorry, Jed," one of the men mumbled.

Longarm said, "I'm the one who started the talk. Sorry, Ashcroft."

The foreman waved a hand. "Aw, hell, Long, you're a stranger in these parts. Can't blame you for bein' curious."

"If I was curious enough to have a look at Salem Valley for myself, where would I find it?" That was the most important question he had asked so far, thought Longarm.

The other men hesitated before answering, clearly not wanting to rile Ashcroft any more.

"You ain't really goin' over there, are you?" Ashcroft asked Longarm.

"Nope." Longarm grinned ruefully. "Truth is, I was sort of thinking I might want to avoid the place entirely. Didn't want to stumble into it accidental-like."

"Well, in that case . . . when you leave here, head west

toward Greybull. Just don't go north toward Black Butte. That's where an arm of the Bighorns juts out from the main range. Salem Valley is below Black Butte."

"Thanks," Longarm said with a nod. "I'll steer well clear of it."

He didn't like lying to simple, honest cowhands such as these men. There'd been a time when Longarm himself had been one of them, cowboying for a living after he'd come out to the frontier from West-by-God Virginia.

But now that he knew where to look for Salem Valley, he would definitely pay it a visit.

Horse Collar Jones's breakfast was just as good as his supper had been, maybe even better. Longarm lingered over a third cup of coffee, then went to the corral to saddle his horse.

He found Harley Kincaid there. "Movin' on?" the young man asked.

"I reckon so. Sure do appreciate your hospitality."

Harley nodded. "Stop by any time, if you're back in these parts."

"I'll do that," promised Longarm with a grin, "if only to eat some more of Horse Collar's cooking!"

A few minutes later, as Longarm led the dun out of the corral, he said to Harley, "I hope your pa sees fit to file his claim on the ranch. I've heard tell of folks in other places who lost their land because they didn't."

"Nick and I will keep trying to convince him," Harley said. "It's not going to be easy, though. When Pa first came out here, there was no such thing as barbed wire or surveys or claims to be filed. There was just a bunch of land, there for whoever could hold it and use it the best."

Longarm swung up into the saddle and then nodded. "Times've changed, all right," he agreed. "So long, Harley."

He left the MK, riding west toward Greybull as Jed Ashcroft had told him to do. When he was well out of sight of the ranch, however, he turned the dun to the north.

Longarm could see the dark, flat, upthrust mass of Black Butte in the distance, surrounded by the more traditional snowcapped peaks of the Bighorns. Using the butte to steer by, he set a fast pace toward it.

By mid-morning, the butte didn't seem any closer, but by noon he was finally closing in on it. He was still on Kincaid range, he knew, because he had seen the MK brand on some of the cattle he had come across during the morning. He hadn't seen any of the Kincaid riders, though.

The sky overhead was mostly clear today, letting some warm, welcome sunshine come through. Gray clouds still boiled to the north, however. They seemed to cast a pall over the mountains, especially Black Butte.

The terrain grew more rugged, but Longarm found a creek that flowed from the general direction he wanted to go and followed it. Sometimes rock walls closed in so that he had to ride in the stream itself. The dun didn't like that very much because the water was very cold.

He came out onto a long, wide bench of land, and on the far side of it, backed up against a line of sheer, dark cliffs, was a cabin. Tendrils of smoke rose from the stone chimney. Somebody was at home.

Longarm wondered if this was the small ranch belonging to Beth Crawford. He reined in and twisted around in the saddle to get his bearings. He was almost directly north of the MK headquarters, he decided. That had to be the Crawford place.

He didn't see any sign of Salem Valley, though.

Longarm put the dun into a walk toward the cabin. The valley was supposed to be hard to find, he reminded himself.

As he came closer, he could make out a cleft in the rock face of the cliff behind the cabin. That could be it, he decided. That could be a passage leading through the cliffs to Salem Valley.

If that were the case, it would make a good hideout for an outlaw gang. A couple of men with rifles could easily defend that entrance.

He wasn't ready to go busting in there just yet, however. If Bull Stennett and the rest of the outlaws were there, a damn-fool play like that would just get him killed. He had to do some scouting first.

And he had to admit, he was curious about Beth Crawford. He wanted to get a look at the so-called "witch woman" for himself.

As he rode closer to the cabin, he saw a gray-and-white cat sitting on a barrel outside the open door. The cat hopped down and ran inside as if scared by Longarm's approach.

A moment later, an old man stepped out of the cabin. He was carrying a shotgun that looked almost as ancient as he was, but the weapon was clean and obviously well cared for. Longarm didn't doubt that it would shoot just fine.

The old man lifted the shotgun when Longarm was about twenty yards away from the cabin. "That's far enough, mister!" he called. "Don't come no closer!"

Longarm reined in and held both hands half lifted to show that he meant no harm. "Take it easy, old-timer," he said. "I'm not looking for trouble."

"What are you lookin' for, then?"

"Is this the Crawford place?"

"What if it is?"

"I was told you might be hiring a hand or two."

"Whoever told you that was too damn stupid to live! We ain't hirin'. Now git!"

"Then this *is* the Crawford ranch?" Longarm persisted.

"That's right," a woman's voice said from beside him.

Longarm's head jerked around. How in blazes had a woman been able to come up alongside him like that without him noticing? Especially since she was on horseback, riding a big black gelding that looked like too much horse for a little thing like her to control.

She wasn't much more than a girl, nineteen or maybe twenty years old. She wore a man's denim trousers rolled up several times at the cuff, a flannel shirt, and a black hat with a floppy brim. Several strands of the honey-blond hair that had been tucked up underneath the hat had escaped and were dangling around her wholesomely pretty face.

"This is the Crawford spread," the young woman went on. "Who were you looking for?"

"Dang it, Melinda," the old man called, "I already done told this feller to rustle his hocks outta here!"

"It's all right, Buck," she told him. "He doesn't look dangerous to me."

The old man called Buck snorted. "That's 'cause you ain't old enough to know dangerous when you see it, gal," he muttered, loudly enough for Longarm to hear him.

Longarm looked at the young woman again and remembered something he had heard from one of the punchers in the MK bunkhouse the night before. "You must be the niece," he said.

"Oh, you're looking for Aunt Beth," Melinda Crawford said. She lowered her voice and added confidentially, "She's a witch, you know."

8

For a second Longarm thought he must have heard the young woman incorrectly, but then the old man yelped, "Dang it, gal, you know you ain't supposed to say things like that!"

"Why not?" Melinda Crawford asked. "You know that's what everybody around here believes anyway."

Longarm asked, "Are you saying that your aunt *ain't* a witch?"

"Of course not! Did you ever hear of anything so ridiculous in your life?" She held out her hand. "We haven't been properly introduced, by the way. I'm Melinda Crawford."

"Custis Long," Longarm told her as he shook her hand. Her grip was firm, and her palm had a few calluses that meant she had worked quite a bit with a rope. Her skin wasn't roughened up like that of many frontier women, however, telling Longarm that she hadn't been at it for too many years.

"Pleased to meet you, Mr. Long," Melinda said. "We don't get many visitors around here anymore, not since people have gotten so scared."

"Scared of what?" asked Longarm.

He glanced toward the old man and saw that Buck had

lowered the shotgun but was still watching him with a glare of dislike.

"Why, the curse, of course," said Melinda. "That goes with my aunt being a witch."

"Which is ridiculous," Longarm said slowly.

"That's right."

"So there's no curse, either?"

"What do you think?"

Longarm thought this pretty young woman didn't look like anybody who would be mixed up with a notorious owlhoot and killer like Bull Stennett. But you never could tell about such things.

"I reckon I'll wait and see what happens," he said. "If bad luck starts following me around, I'll know who to blame it on."

Melinda laughed. "I don't know what you're looking for, Mr. Long, but I'm glad you didn't get scared off by a lot of nonsense."

"Looking for work," said Longarm, but before he could get any farther, the old man interrupted him.

"I done told him we ain't hirin'," Buck said. "Leave him go on about his business, Melinda."

"Without offering him a cup of coffee and some grub?" Melinda shook her head. "I don't think so."

She swung down off her horse, and as she did so, Longarm couldn't help but admire the way her denim trousers stretched tautly over her rounded rump. Her breasts were nice, too, pushing against the fabric of the man's shirt she wore. She managed to look innocent and sensual at the same time, a rare but potent combination.

Longarm dismounted, too, ignoring the glares sent in his direction by the old man. Melinda said, "Take care of the horses, would you, please, Buck?" and the old-timer snorted. He set the shotgun aside and took the reins of both mounts, however.

Melinda led Longarm into the cabin. It was neatly kept and the puncheon floor had been recently swept. A rough-hewn table was in the center of the room, a black cast-iron stove in the corner. A blanket partition closed off what was probably the sleeping area for the two women.

Longarm noticed that the gray-and-white cat he had seen run into the cabin earlier was gone. The animal must have jumped out one of the two windows, he decided.

He also noticed that several shelves made of planks had been attached to the walls, and they were full of knick-knacks. He saw several small, carved, exotic-looking figurines, and tiny wooden chests, and little metal stars, and bits of colored glass arranged in intricate but somehow odd patterns. . . .

Longarm was used to seeing guns and Indian rugs hung on cabin walls, but he had never encountered anything quite like this before.

"You've noticed my aunt's collection," Melinda said, still smiling as she took off her jacket and hat and hung them on nails beside the door.

"Collection of what?" asked Longarm.

"Objets d'art, she would call them. Art objects. She was educated in Paris, you know, and she began her collection while she was in Europe. None of these pieces are very valuable, though. They're mainly just things she likes."

"How'd an art collector from Paris wind up in the Bighorn Basin in Wyoming?" Longarm was so puzzled that he asked the question anyway, even though he knew it might be rude.

"Oh, Aunt Beth isn't *from* Paris," replied Melinda as she went to the stove and touched the pot of coffee sitting there to see if it was hot. "She was born in Kansas, just like me. But she took the fancy of a rich man in the town where we lived, and he paid to have her go to college over there." Melinda lowered her voice and grinned as she went on, "I think she was his mistress, but she won't talk about that. She thinks I'm too sheltered to know about such things."

Longarm shrugged. This was all going a little fast, but

49

so far he hadn't heard anything that would make him think there was a connection between Beth Crawford and Bull Stennett.

Melinda poured coffee into a couple of cups and set them on the table. She and Longarm sat down across from each other.

"Aunt Beth lived in Boston and Philadelphia for a while when she came back from Paris, and then when my folks died she came back to Kansas to take care of me." Melinda mentioned her parents' deaths matter-of-factly, and Longarm supposed some time had passed since they had occurred. "There was some sort of trouble and we had to leave town. A falling-out between Aunt Beth and her former paramour, I suspect. We heard of some land here that we could homestead, so we decided to give ranching a try. We've been here for a couple of years now, and it seems to be going all right."

"Where'd you come up with that old pelican outside?"

Melinda laughed. "You mean Buck? I suppose you could call him an old family retainer."

That seemed to be all the answer she was going to give to Longarm's question, and he didn't really care where the two women had found the crotchety old-timer. Melinda was the talkative sort, like Harley Kincaid, so he decided to try to find out a little more.

"I've heard plenty of talk that the valley behind here is supposed to be cursed, all right," he said. "How'd that get started?"

"I honestly don't know. It's a wild, rugged, dangerous place, and I suppose some men have ridden up into it and had accidents of some sort. Whenever anyone comes along who wants to ride through the cliffs into the valley, we warn them not to, but sometimes they don't listen."

"Through the cliffs?" repeated Longarm.

"Yes, there's a little passage. It winds back and forth a lot, and it's very narrow in places. Sometimes rocks fall from up above, and I wouldn't be surprised if someday the passage is blocked. Just getting into Salem Valley is dangerous."

"Have you ever been there?"

Solemnly, Melinda shook her head. "No, Aunt Beth explored up that way not long after we came here—she's very daring, you know—and she's forbidden me to go into the passage. All I know is what she's told me, but that's enough."

Longarm sipped the coffee. It was good, but not as tasty as what Horse Collar Jones made.

"Sounds like a good place to stay away from, all right," he said. "That's what they told me down on the Kincaid spread."

Melinda made a face. "You've been to the MK? Then I'm not surprised you've heard all about witches and curses and the like. They're not very friendly down there."

"Martin Kincaid thinks you and your aunt want to push onto his land." Longarm didn't say anything about Kincaid's claim to the MK ranch evidently not being a proper one. He didn't want to put ideas into anybody's head and cause problems for Kincaid.

Melinda shook her head and said, "That's crazy. How could just the three of us handle any more land than we have now?"

Longarm smiled. "Maybe that's why you need to hire somebody like me to ride for you."

For the first time, the young woman looked slightly suspicious of him. "I don't think so," she said slowly. "I've been talking an awful lot, haven't I? How do you get people to open up to you like that, Mr. Long?"

Longarm chuckled and said, "Must be this honest face of mine. Folks just naturally like to talk to me."

"Well, I've probably said too much." Melinda stood up. "There are biscuits and beans I can warm for lunch. Aunt Beth will be here any minute. You can eat with us, Mr. Long, but then it might be best if you moved on, since you don't have any real business to keep you here."

"Sure," Longarm responded agreeably. He didn't know what he'd said to put Melinda's back up. As long as she was getting proddy, though, maybe he would push a little more and see what happened. "Maybe I'll take a ride up into Salem Valley."

Melinda turned sharply toward him. "Don't do that," she said, again reminding him of Harley Kincaid. "Something might happen to you, and then I'd feel like it was my fault for not stopping you."

"Everybody keeps telling me that," said Longarm, "but I've ridden some rough trails in my time. I don't reckon there's anything up there I haven't seen before."

"I wouldn't be too sure of that," said Melinda. She was frowning worriedly at him now.

Longarm shrugged again. "I never like to worry a pretty lady," he said. "I guess I can steer clear of Salem Valley."

That wasn't his intention at all, but Melinda Crawford didn't have to know that.

She went on preparing the meal while Longarm sat at the table and sipped coffee. After a few minutes of silence, he said, "Where is your aunt, anyway?"

"She rode over to check the stock in our west pasture," replied Melinda. "I looked in on the east pasture this morning, but it's closer so I got back first."

"Do you have enough graze to last the winter?"

"Last winter was all right," the young woman said. "That was the first one we'd spent here. Black Butte protects us some from the bad weather, so the snow isn't as deep here as it is elsewhere. Unless there's a real blizzard, the cattle will be able to get to the grass that's left. And we have some hay put up in the barn. We'll make it just fine."

Longarm thought the confidence he heard in Melinda's voice wasn't completely sincere. Running a ranch, even a small one such as this one, had to be a daunting task for a couple of women. And Wyoming winters could be rough enough to put the fear of God into anybody, male or female. Melinda seemed brave enough, but she would probably be glad when spring came again.

The smell of biscuits and beans filled the cabin as the food heated, and Longarm realized he was hungry. It had been quite a while since his breakfast at the MK that morning. He was looking forward to the food when he heard the sound of hoofbeats outside. That would be Beth Crawford returning to the cabin from the west pasture, he supposed.

The hoofbeats stopped, and he heard low voices outside. The old-timer called Buck was telling his employer about the stranger who had ridden up earlier, guessed Longarm.

A moment later, a woman stepped into the doorway. For a witch, she was mighty pretty, he thought. But he supposed she wasn't a real witch after all, because if she was she could have cast some sort of spell on him . . .

Instead of pointing a gun at him and asking, grim-faced, "What the hell are you doing here, mister?"

9

Melinda turned from the stove, gasping as she saw the revolver in the other woman's fist. "Aunt Beth!" she exclaimed, confirming Longarm's speculation about the newcomer's identity. "There's no need to do that! Mr. Long doesn't mean us any harm."

"How do you know that?" demanded Beth Crawford. "He could a thief or a murderer. He could even be a spy sent up here by that bastard Kincaid."

Melinda's eyes narrowed as she looked again at Longarm. "He *did* admit that he'd been to the MK. . . ."

"Riding the chuck line, that's all," said Longarm, forcing himself to appear calm and relaxed. He didn't like having anyone point a gun at him, even a female as nice looking as Beth Crawford.

Melinda's aunt was in her early thirties, Longarm guessed, with fairly short blond hair that was a shade lighter than her niece's honey-colored hair. Beth's eyes, like Melinda's, were blue and sharply intelligent. She wore a brown hat and a matching vest over a white shirt. Her riding skirt was the same color as the hat and vest. A shell belt and holster were strapped around her hips.

Longarm couldn't help but notice that the aunt's breasts were just a touch bigger than the niece's. This wasn't really the right time to be making such comparisons, he supposed, but some habits were hard to break.

"Martin Kincaid didn't send you up here to cause trouble for us?" Beth Crawford snapped.

"Nope," replied Longarm. "But if he had, would you expect me to tell the truth about it?"

She looked intently at him for a moment, then her full lips abruptly curved in a smile that made her even prettier. "No, I suppose I wouldn't," she said. "But somehow, after getting a good look at you, you don't strike me as a troublemaker after all, Mr. . . . . Long, was it?"

"Custis Long, ma'am," Longarm said with a pleasant nod. As Beth lowered the pistol, he got to his feet, a move he had postponed until now because he wasn't sure how itchy her trigger finger might be. He extended his hand to her. "Pleased to make your acquaintance."

Beth holstered the gun and shook hands with him. Her palm was rougher than Melinda's, indicating to Longarm that she spent more time handling a rope than the younger woman. Her grip was firm and warm and very nice, though.

Melinda still looked a little suspicious. "Mr. Long is full of questions about this area, Aunt Beth," she commented.

Beth arched an eyebrow. "Is that so, Mr. Long?" As an afterthought, she waved at the table and added, "Please, sit down again."

Longarm sat and said, "Sorry if I seem a mite inquisitive, ladies. When a fella's been on the trail for a long time, spending most of his days by himself, he likes to talk whenever he's around other folks. Especially when those folks are a couple of ladies as pretty as the two of you."

"Flattery will get you exactly nowhere, Mr. Long," Beth said tartly as she took off her hat and hung it on a nail next to the one where Melinda's was hung. Longarm had set his Stetson on the table when he came in. "You already have your cup of coffee," Beth went on, "and Melinda will have the food ready soon. That's all you'll get on the Circle Moon, I'm afraid."

"The Circle Moon," Longarm repeated. "That's your brand?"

"That's right. Most people think it's just one circle inside another, but Melinda and I know better."

"Reckon you can call your brand anything you want, so long as you register it," Longarm said with a shrug. "And file a proper claim on your land."

"Which is exactly what we did when we homesteaded this place," Beth said as she poured some coffee for herself and then came to the table to sit down opposite Longarm.

That was interesting, he mused. The women had done things proper and filed on their land, unlike Martin Kincaid. If they wanted to, they could file on some of the MK range as well. That was what Kincaid feared. So far during this visit, however, Longarm had seen no sign that either Melinda or her aunt were that land hungry.

Such things had nothing to do with his job here, he reminded himself. Making his voice sound just idly curious, he said, "You must not see many strangers around here. Miss Melinda said it had been a while since you'd had visitors."

Melinda made a face again. "Ugh. Don't call me Miss Melinda, please. Make it just Melinda."

"We don't have many visitors," agreed Beth. "There's really no reason for anyone to come out here. There's no trail that leads through to anywhere."

"Except Salem Valley," Longarm said. "And it's cursed."

Beth shot a sharp glance at her niece. "Melinda, have you been spreading those stories again?"

Melinda brought a pot of beans and a pan of biscuits from the stove and set them on the table. Defensively, she said, "He already knew about the so-called curse, Aunt Beth. Remember, he's been down at the MK. You know how those cowboys like to talk nonsense."

"And that's all it is, nonsense," Beth said as she looked again at Longarm. "There's no such thing as a curse. And I'm *not* a witch, no matter what some people say."

Longarm grinned and held his hands up, palms out. "I ain't one to accuse folks," he said. "I just heard stories, that's all. I figure a wild yarn usually doesn't amount to a hill of beans."

"Well, then, you're one of the intelligent ones." Beth reached for the spoon in the pot and began dishing out beans into the plates that Melinda brought to the table. "Most people around here will believe anything, the wilder the yarn the better."

Melinda went to the door and opened it, stepping out to call, "Buck! Grub is ready, Buck! Buck, where are you?" When there was no response, she turned to her aunt and said, "Buck's not out here, Aunt Beth."

"Oh, you know how he is," Beth said, "always chasing after something. He'll come back when he's good and ready, Melinda, don't worry."

Melinda shrugged and closed the door, then came to the table and sat down in the chair at the end. For the next few minutes, the three of them ate in silence, washing down the beans and biscuits with coffee.

Finally, Melinda said, "Where will you go from here, Mr. Long?"

"Might try to get on up to Montana before the snow flies."

"You'll have to hurry," said Beth. "And you won't find the ranches up there hiring, either."

Longarm shrugged. "Well, I may have to give up on finding a riding job and go to clerking in a store or something."

Beth looked at him for a long moment, her blue-eyed gaze intense. Then she said, "No, I don't think so. I just can't see you wearing an apron and standing behind a counter, Mr. Long. You're too active a man for that sort of life."

"No offense, ma'am, but how do you know just how active I am?"

Beth smiled. "A woman can tell things about a man." She laughed. "I'm just glad the opposite isn't true."

Longarm wasn't so sure of that. He could tell a little about Beth Crawford by looking in her eyes. He could see the interest that had started growing there after her initial suspicions of him were put to rest.

A woman in the prime of life, like Beth, who was stuck out in the middle of nowhere with only her niece and an old man for company . . . well, a woman like that couldn't help but be interested when a man like Longarm rode in. He knew that, and under other circumstances, he might have tried to get to know Beth a little better. She was mighty good looking.

But he had come up here to do a job, and that meant finding Bull Stennett and the rest of the boss outlaw's gang. He tried to steer the conversation back in that direction by asking, "Does anybody ever try to slip past this place up into Salem Valley?"

"Why would anyone want to do that?" asked Beth. "There's nothing up there."

"Nothing at all? What about grass and water?"

"Well, I suppose there is. I haven't really explored the whole place. But there's only one way in, and that's through the cleft in the cliffs. You might have seen it as you were riding in."

Longarm nodded.

"Can you imagine how long it would take to drive a herd of cattle through such a narrow passage? In places they'd have to go through one at a time." Beth shook her head. "No, I just don't think it would be worth the time and trouble it would take to bring any cattle in there."

But a gang of desperadoes like Stennett's bunch wouldn't need any cows, thought Longarm. As long as they could make it through the cliffs and defend the passage in case any lawmen discovered them, that was all that would matter to them.

And it would be easy enough to slip in and out of Salem Valley at night, so that Beth and Melinda wouldn't know anything about it. If that was the case, Salem Valley could be serving as Stennett's hideout without the two women being aware of it at all.

Longarm hoped he wasn't letting his instinctive liking for Beth and Melinda color his judgment. It was entirely possible they *were* connected to the outlaws. But Longarm didn't think so, and his years as a star packer had made him a pretty good judge of character.

His plan all along had been to take a look for himself in Salem Valley, and he hadn't learned anything here on the Circle Moon to change his mind. He didn't want to ride up there in broad daylight, though.

When he had finished eating, he sighed appreciatively, drained the rest of the coffee in his cup, and said, "Well, I reckon I'd better be riding on."

"So soon?" Beth said.

"I'll make a few more miles toward Montana."

"In that case, we have some bread and some roast beef. Melinda, will you make Mr. Long some sandwiches he can take with him?"

"Sure," Melinda said.

"I appreciate that," said Longarm. "Thank you both."

"You wouldn't happen to be going back down toward the MK first, would you?" asked Beth.

"Nope, wasn't planning to. Why?"

"I just thought you might take a message to Martin Kincaid for me. I'd really like to tell him that he has nothing to fear from us, and I wish he and his men would just leave us alone."

Longarm frowned slightly. "The MK riders have been giving you trouble?"

"Nothing too terrible, I suppose. Back during the summer one of our ponds was fouled, and we've missed a few head of cattle now and then. I know it's not simple rustling—Kincaid's herd is ten or twenty times the size of ours to start with—so I suspect they're just trying to annoy us into giving up the Circle Moon."

Longarm scraped a thumbnail along the line of his jaw

as his frown deepened. "That's what it sounds like," he agreed. "Don't know that I'll ever cross trails with Kincaid again, or if he'd even listen to a drifter like me, but if I see him, I'll sure give him your message."

"Thank you, Mr. Long."

Melinda put a canvas pouch on the table. "Here are the sandwiches," she said.

Longarm got to his feet. "I'm much obliged, ladies. You've sure brightened this old cowboy's day."

"You're not old, Mr. Long," Melinda said. "You're just . . . seasoned."

Longarm threw back his head and laughed. "Yep, I reckon I am."

He put on his hat, picked up the bag of sandwiches, and left the cabin. Beth and Melinda came to the doorway behind him. His horse was hitched to a post near the barn, and as Longarm walked over to the dun, he saw the gray-and-white cat again, sitting just inside the open barn door. The animal was giving him a feline glare that reminded him of something, but he couldn't say just what it was.

He untied the dun's reins, swung up into the saddle, and turned the horse to wave a farewell to the two women. They stood in the doorway of the cabin and returned the wave, the afternoon sunlight shining on their blond hair.

"A mighty pretty pair," Longarm muttered to himself as he put the dun into a trot that carried them away from the cabin. "Yes, sir, mighty pretty."

Then he put all thoughts of Beth and Melinda Crawford out of his head. Back there behind the cabin in the looming cliffs, the trail to the mysterious hidden valley waited for him. He would have to postpone his visit until after dark, but soon, he vowed, he would find out for himself what was up there.

Curse or no curse, he was riding to Salem Valley tonight.

10

Longarm rode well out of sight of the cabin, then turned the dun north, angling deeper into the foothills below Black Butte. He found himself a nice spot to pass the afternoon and hobbled the horse so that it could graze while he dozed underneath a pine tree on a bed of fallen needles.

He didn't mean to fall sound asleep, but that was what happened. As he slumbered on the Wyoming hillside with his hat pulled down and the collar of his sheepskin jacket up around his ears, Longarm dreamed.

Not surprisingly, Beth Crawford and her niece Melinda played parts in his dream. He saw them wearing black dresses and high-peaked black hats, and although their bodies were bent and twisted like old women, their faces were still young and beautiful.

They were using long wooden poles to stir something in a big, black cast-iron pot. A cauldron, that was what it was called, Longarm remembered. And it was big enough that a gent could fit inside it, which was exactly where he found himself, neck deep in hot water as the Crawford women poked at him with their poles.

Melinda laughed and said loudly, "Double, double, toil and trouble!"

"Fire burn and cauldron bubble!" added Beth with a laugh of her own.

Longarm recognized those words from somewhere, but under the circumstances he didn't think he ought to waste time trying to remember their source. Instead, he called to the two women, "Hold on there, dadgum it! It's getting pretty hot in here."

"Eye of newt—" Melinda began, ignoring him.

Longarm had had enough. He started to climb out of the pot, but as he emerged from the water he realized he was naked. Beth poked at his privates with her pole, and he jumped back, falling into the hot water with a splash.

"Son of a bitch!" he yelped.

Suddenly he remembered where he had seen something like this in the past. He'd once attended a performance of Shakespeare's play *Macbeth* at the Denver Opera House in company with a pretty young woman who liked such things, and he knew now that this was similar to a scene from that production.

In the play, though, there had been three witches, not two, and they'd been made up to look mighty ugly, not like Beth and Melinda at all. And there sure as hell hadn't been a deputy United States marshal cooking in the pot.

Longarm grabbed the sides of the cauldron and tried to heave himself out again. This time somebody grabbed him from behind and shoved him down so that his head went under the water. He came up dripping and sputtering and looked around.

Tom Morgan stood there laughing at him, the front of the outlaw's shirt all bloody and his face torn up where the wolves had gotten at him after pulling him out of the shallow grave where Longarm had left him. He pointed at Longarm in the pot and guffawed, and the redheaded whore, Donna, came up beside him and started fondling him while she laughed at Longarm, too.

A shotgun roared, and Longarm jerked around at the sound to see the old-timer called Buck standing there holding a greener. Powder smoke curled from one of the barrels of the weapon. Buck said in a hollow voice, "I got one barrel left for you, Marshal," and then slowly brought the shotgun to bear on Longarm. As he squinted over the double barrels, Buck grinned, and his teeth were all sharp and pointy and not human at all.

Orange flame exploded from the second barrel of the shotgun and filled Longarm's face, and he woke up with a shout, his hand going to the butt of his own gun. He jerked the Colt from its holster and looked around wildly for something at which to shoot.

The hillside was empty and peaceful except for the dun. The horse looked at him curiously, obviously puzzled by the way Longarm had let out a yell for no apparent reason.

Longarm took a deep breath and then slid the Colt back into leather. He scrubbed a hand over his face and shook his head.

Normally, he wasn't one to remember his dreams, but this one had been so vivid that he couldn't shake the images it had left behind. The whole thing didn't make a lick of sense, of course. But then, dreams rarely did.

Still, this one had been really loco.

Longarm stepped out from under the pine and looked up at the sky. The clouds that had been to the north earlier in the day had moved down some, and they were about to swallow up the sun that was low in the western sky.

Darkness would come a little earlier than usual tonight, and that suited Longarm just fine. He wouldn't have to wait much longer before starting for Salem Valley.

And while he waited he would stay awake, because he sure as blazes didn't want to fall asleep—and dream—again.

With clouds covering the moon and stars, the night was extremely dark. That was all right with Longarm. He had studied the landscape closely as he rode away from the Crawford ranch earlier that day, and although he had to

63

take it slow, he was able to guide the dun back toward the beetling cliffs without much trouble.

A light was burning in the cabin, a faint glow escaping around the shutters over the windows. That was enough to allow Longarm to steer clear of the place. When he was close enough to see the light, he swung down from the saddle and led the horse by the reins as he walked toward the cliffs.

A couple of times he had to stop and look back at the cabin to get his bearings, but eventually he found the cleft in the rock face that led to Salem Valley. At least, he hoped it was the right passage. He hadn't seen any other openings when he studied the cliffs that afternoon.

If it had been dark out in the open, it was truly black as the pits of Hades in here, thought Longarm as he moved into the passage, still leading the dun. He held the reins in his left hand and kept his right stretched out in front of him to warn him when the cleft turned and twisted. Even so he ran into the rock walls several times.

It's like it was laid out by a drunk on a blind mule, Longarm told himself as he made his slow, laborious way through the passage. He walked as quietly as possible, but from time to time he kicked a rock that made noise as it rolled along the floor of the cleft, and the steel-shod hooves of the dun produced an occasional ringing sound as they struck the stony ground.

If Stennett's gang was in there and had a lookout posted, they might know he was coming, Longarm mused. He had to hope the valley's isolation was so complete that Stennett and the other outlaws had grown overconfident about not being discovered.

After what seemed like an hour of following the passage's bends and loops—and at times it was so narrow that it almost pressed on both of Longarm's shoulders—he sensed more than saw the rock walls falling away on either side of him. As if they had been waiting for the right time, the clouds parted slightly as Longarm stepped out of the cleft. A few slivers of moonlight peeked through the opening.

That was enough illumination for Longarm to see that he stood at the head of a small valley about half a mile wide and maybe three miles long. It was completely surrounded by tall, jagged peaks that would be next to impossible to climb, meaning the only practical way in and out was through the passage at Longarm's back.

A dark line of vegetation meandered roughly through the center of the valley. That marked the course of a stream, Longarm decided. Probably a tiny creek that emerged from under a rock wall and went back under another on the far side of the valley. But it would provide enough water for men and horses, if not for a herd of cattle.

Longarm's pulse beat a little faster. He was growing more and more confident that he had discovered the hideout of the Bull Stennett gang. The fact that he had made it this far without being challenged likely meant there was no sentry standing watch over the trail through the cliffs.

His keen eyes scanned every foot of the valley that he could see from here. If he had been able to spot a light or anything else to indicate the presence of human beings, that might have been enough to convince him he had found his goal.

But the valley appeared to be totally dark, and Longarm knew he couldn't just assume that Stennett and the rest of the gang—minus Tom Morgan—were here. He would have to wait until morning to get proof.

Once he had it, though, he could start trying to figure out how to apprehend the outlaws. He couldn't just ride in shooting; there would be too many of them. There was probably a telegraph office in Greybull, since it was the county seat. He could wire Billy Vail to send him some reinforcements.

Or he could buy some dynamite and blow the passage through the cliffs closed. That would effectively trap Stennett's gang inside the valley until spring, when a way could be dug through to them.

Of course, the outlaws might have starved to death by then, depending on how many provisions they had, so Longarm decided that might not be the best idea after all.

The first step was to wait until morning, so that he could confirm the presence of Stennett's gang. He moved back into the cleft, taking the dun with him.

Longarm stopped after he had gone a few yards. He and the horse would be invisible from the valley as long as they stayed here. He ground-hitched the dun and found a rock to sit on.

It was going to be a long, cold wait until morning.

Longarm huddled in the sheepskin jacket, keeping his hands buried in the pockets. His fingers started to get numb anyway, so he took his hands out and rubbed them together. His breath fogged thickly in front of his face, but then he couldn't see it anymore because the rift in the clouds closed and the darkness was complete again.

Longarm had endured a lot of cold nights in his life, but he would remember this as one of the worst. His muscles ached and stiffened, and his feet felt like chunks of ice in his boots. From time to time he walked around and flapped his arms in an attempt to increase his circulation, but that helped only slightly.

There was no way for him to tell how many hours had passed. He couldn't judge time in a situation such as this, and it was too dark to look at his watch. It felt like he'd been hiding in this frigid cleft in the rock for a week at least, although he knew that was crazy.

Sometime, along toward morning, it began to snow.

The nap he'd had the previous afternoon hadn't been a restful one, and he found himself getting sleepy. Dozing off would be a real danger this time; he wouldn't be risking just a nightmare. If the snow got heavier, he could freeze to death, or one of the outlaws could stumble over him. . . .

Although what anybody in his right mind would be doing outside on a night like this . . .

Longarm's head drooped toward his chest as he leaned against a boulder.

The faint scrape of leather on rock woke him.

His head jerked up and he twisted instinctively toward the sound that had warned him. His hand flashed across his body and palmed out the Colt.

The sound of a shot suddenly slammed against the walls of the passage, echoing painfully. The bright glare of flame geysering from the barrel of a gun partially blinded Longarm, but he was able to snap a shot in return at the muzzle flash as he dropped to a knee.

The other gun crashed again, setting off more echoes, and this time a giant fist struck Longarm in the head. He felt himself falling over backward. He tried to fire again, but the Colt was no longer in his hand. He couldn't even feel his hand.

Or anything else, for that matter. He was out cold by the time he hit the ground.

11

Longarm moved his head, and pain exploded through it. That told him he was still alive, but the relief he felt at that discovery didn't stop him from letting out a groan.

Light assaulted his eyes as he tried to open them. He squeezed them shut again as he instinctively tried to turn away from the light. The movement set off fresh explosions of agony inside his skull.

Sound grated against his ears, strange and distorted. After a moment the noise became less harsh, and then it gradually turned into a voice.

A woman's voice, soft and musical.

"You're alive. Thank goodness! Don't move, Mr. Long. Just stay right there!"

Longarm wasn't sure where he was going to go in his current condition. Budging the least little bit made his head feel as if it were going to split right in two like an overripe watermelon.

He was beginning to realize that he was lying on his back on something fairly soft. It felt good, or at least would have felt good under other circumstances. He heard Melinda Crawford hurry away somewhere. He had recognized her voice and figured he was in the cabin that served as headquarters of the Circle Moon ranch.

Lying as still as he possibly could with his eyes squeezed shut, Longarm tried to force his brain to work. In bits and pieces, his memory came back to him. He recalled something about an odd dream, and a narrow place that was dark and cold, and then the bright flare of a gun's muzzle blast . . .

Maybe it had all been a dream, he told himself. Maybe none of it had happened.

But that wouldn't account for the fact that he was lying here with his head hurting like blazes. And Melinda had sounded a little surprised that he was still alive.

He'd been shot, he realized. Someone had sneaked up on him in the passage through the cliffs—he remembered now that was where he had been, waiting for morning so that he could get a better look at Salem Valley—and started shooting at him. He had tried to return the fire, and then he'd been hit.

Melinda was right. He was damned lucky to still be alive, Longarm told himself.

Footsteps approached him, and a cool cloth was laid on his forehead. He winced. This time moving didn't make his head ache quite so badly.

"You were right, Melinda," Beth Crawford said. "Mr. Long is indeed alive. Welcome back to the land of the living, Mr. Long."

Longarm felt compelled to try opening his eyes again. He lifted the lids just a fraction of an inch. Light stabbed at him again.

"Blow out that candle, Melinda."

"Yes, Aunt Beth."

Longarm heard Melinda's breath as she blew out the candle. He risked opening his eyes for a third time, and this time the room was blessedly dim around him. As he pried his eyelids up some more, a blurry shape came into view above him. After a moment it resolved itself into Beth Crawford's face, which wore a concerned frown.

"There, that should be better," she said. "I'm not surprised the light bothered you after you were unconscious for so long."

That didn't sound too good, thought Longarm. He wondered just how long he had been out cold. He opened his mouth to try to form the question on his lips, but his tongue was dry and lumpy and wouldn't cooperate.

"Wait just a minute," Beth told him. "Melinda, fetch a dipper of water."

"Right away."

Again Longarm heard the younger woman hurry out of the room. His eyesight was improving, and he realized now that he was lying on a bunk in the cabin, behind the blanket partition. That meant he had taken either Melinda's or Beth's bed.

At the moment, he didn't care about putting one of the women out of her bunk. He was too tired, and hurt too much to worry about being a gentleman.

Melinda came back a minute later. Beth took the tin dipper from her and held it to Longarm's mouth as she gingerly supported his head with her other hand.

"Try to drink a little," she urged him.

Longarm didn't want to disappoint her. He took a tiny sip of the water, which was cold and clear and tasted incredibly delicious to him, every bit as good as a slug of Maryland rye ever had. Since he'd had one sip, he took another, a little bigger this time.

Then his stomach clenched as the water hit it and came back up. He turned his head to the side as he retched, embarrassed at being sick in front of the women.

"That's all right, Mr. Long," Beth told him. "An upset stomach is common when someone has a concussion, which I'm sure you do after that rock fell on your head."

"I told him it was dangerous in there and that rocks sometimes fell like that," said Melinda.

Even through his sickness, Longarm knew that what he had just heard the women say was all wrong. No rock had fallen on him. Somebody had shot him. The bullet must have just grazed his skull, he decided, since he was still alive, but the damage had definitely been done by a slug.

"Not . . . rock," he managed to rasp.

"What do you mean?" asked Beth. "Of course a rock fell on you. We found it lying right beside you. There was even blood and bits of hair on it where it struck you."

If that was the case, then somebody had walloped him with the rock *after* creasing him, he thought.

And yet, he had no proof of that, he realized. True, someone had been shooting at him when he was hit and blacked out, but it was possible the bushwhacker's second shot had missed, too, just like the first one. A rock *could* have tumbled from the top of the cleft and struck him in the head just as the shadowy gunman fired the second time.

It was a far-fetched idea, thought Longarm, but he couldn't rule it out completely.

He didn't feel like arguing the matter, either. As Beth eased his head back down onto the bunk, he sighed. His head was still pounding to beat the band, but he seemed to be a little stronger now that the sickness had subsided. He said, "How . . . long . . ."

"Were you unconscious?" Beth finished the question for him. "More than two full days. We found you yesterday morning, and it's night now. Goodness knows how long you lay there before we came across you."

Two days. A lot could happen in that amount of time. Whoever had taken those shots at Longarm could be a hundred miles away by now.

Or right here in this room.

As that thought struck him, something stirred guiltily inside Longarm. Beth and Melinda had hauled his unconscious carcass out of that ugly gash in the cliffs and taken care of him, evidently doing their best to nurse him back to health—and here he was suspecting them of shooting him in the first place.

And yet, he had been a lawman for enough years to

71

know that everybody was a suspect until the evidence ruled them in the clear. It was unlikely that either Beth or Melinda had been the bushwhacker—if that was the case, she could have gone ahead and killed him while he was unconscious—but just like the business about the falling rock, he couldn't eliminate the possibility entirely.

He couldn't do anything about it at the moment, either, not in the condition he was in. He said huskily, "I'm much obliged . . . to both of you . . . for taking care of me."

"You shouldn't have ignored our warnings about Salem Valley," Beth said sternly. "We told you it was a dangerous place to go."

"It's . . . cursed." Longarm managed a faint smile as he spoke.

Beth patted his leg familiarly through the covers that were spread over him. "Don't start that nonsense again. The only curse around here is the curiosity that took you up that passage through the cliffs."

"Curiosity killed the cat, they say," put in Melinda, "although I wouldn't let Buck hear that."

So the old-timer liked cats, Longarm thought as he closed his eyes. He wasn't surprised. The crotchety ranch hand and that gray-and-white mouser were two of a kind, sort of lean and scruffy looking with their best days behind them.

"You should rest some more," Beth told Longarm gently. "When you wake up, maybe you'll feel like eating something. You'll need to get your strength back."

"Yes'm," murmured Longarm as he felt drowsiness stealing over him. This was genuine sleep, he sensed, the healing kind instead of the oblivion that had gripped him earlier.

He surrendered to it, hoping that he wouldn't have another of those odd nightmares.

If he dreamed, he didn't remember it, and he was damned grateful for that when he woke up.

His head still ached, but not nearly as bad as it had before. As he opened his eyes and looked around the room, he saw that light was coming around the edges of the drawn blanket. It was too bright for candlelight or lamplight. That was sunshine coming in through a window, he decided. That, and the smell of coffee and bacon in the air, told him it was morning. He had slept the night through.

Which meant that three days had passed now since the women had found him.

He was ravenously hungry, and he would have tried to sit up but then he heard someone else stirring in the room. He turned his head a little and saw that another bunk formed an L with the one he was lying on. Melinda Crawford lay in it, wrapped up in some blankets. She was coming awake, too.

Longarm figured the young woman might be embarrassed if she opened her eyes and caught him watching her, so he rolled his head the other way and kept his breathing regular, as if he were still asleep. He heard Melinda yawn, and then she pushed the covers back. A moment later the bunk creaked a little as she stood up.

Longarm heard the rustle of clothing, and then Melinda said in a half whisper, "It's all right, Mr. Long. I know you're awake."

Longarm turned his head toward her again, just as Melinda reached down to grasp the hem of the thick flannel nightgown she was wearing. She pulled it up and peeled the garment over her head, then dropped it on the bunk, leaving her standing there brazenly nude except for the socks she was wearing.

She smiled down at him as his eyes widened in surprise. The body she displayed so openly was undeniably lovely. Her firm, round breasts were globes of creamy flesh crowned by small, pink nipples. Her belly was flat, and her hips swelled perfectly. The triangle of finespun hair at the juncture of her thighs was the same honey

73

blond as the hair on her head, which was tousled now from sleep. Her thighs and calves were muscular, just made for wrapping around a man as he made love to her.

She posed for him for several seconds, clearly feeling no shame at all. Longarm's shaft hardened, and the pounding ache in his head got worse.

"Damn it, girl," he growled quietly, "I'm in no shape for this." Not to mention the fact that Melinda's aunt could walk in at any time, he added mentally.

"I'm sorry," she whispered. She turned away from him, giving him an enticing view of her exquisitely rounded rump, and began pulling on the bottoms from a pair of long underwear.

Longarm turned his head to the wall and gritted his teeth. Watching a pretty gal get dressed always made him almost as aroused as watching one shed her duds.

After a few minutes, Melinda said, "It's all right now. I'm decent."

She was more than that, thought Longarm.

But he didn't have time to mull over just how pretty Melinda Crawford was, because at that moment, her aunt thrust back the blanket curtain. She had a Winchester gripped in her other hand as she said in a tense voice, "Riders coming."

12

Longarm struggled to sit up. Beth motioned him back down. "It's all right, Mr. Long. Just stay where you are and rest."

"Not if there's trouble coming," said Longarm determinedly. As he came upright, the world spun crazily around him for a moment, but then it righted itself. He threw the covers back, and the cold air in the room made him realize he was naked.

Just like that damned dream, only he wasn't in a pot of hot water this time!

Beth and Melinda both looked away, but not before he caught a glimpse of the smiles on their faces. "I assure you we can handle this, Mr. Long," Beth told him. "I'm not afraid of Martin Kincaid and his men."

So riders from the MK had come to call, thought Longarm. From his brief acquaintance with Martin Kincaid, Longarm didn't believe the rancher was the type of man to start a corpse-and-cartridge session with a couple of women, no matter what the provocation. So as he pulled the covers back over his lower half, he said, "You ladies go on. I'll get dressed, just in case. If you need a hand, sing out."

Beth nodded. "All right, but be careful. I imagine you're still pretty shaky."

That was true enough, Longarm thought as he climbed out of the bunk a few seconds later, after Beth and Melinda had gone into the other part of the cabin and pulled the blanket partition closed behind them. He spotted his long underwear and pants lying on a chair at the end of the bunk and reached for them, only to sway dizzily as he bent over.

Take it slow, Longarm told himself. There was no hurry.

But he could hear the hoofbeats outside now as quite a few horses came pounding up to the cabin, and the sound carried some urgency with it.

The cabin door opened and closed. Longarm grabbed the bottom half of the long underwear and pulled it on, then stepped into his pants and quickly buttoned them. That would have to do for now. Bare chested, with the floor cold against his bare feet, he stepped out into the other part of the cabin and looked around for a weapon in case he needed one.

His saddle and the rest of his gear was lying in a corner, including his Winchester. He stepped over to it and picked up the rifle. His head went a little crazy again, but he conquered the feeling as he checked to make sure the Winchester was loaded.

Longarm moved to the closest window. He unlatched the shutter and eased it back just a tad, enough for him to be able to hear what was going on outside.

"—up here," someone was saying angrily. "What have you done with him?"

That was Martin Kincaid's voice, thought Longarm.

Beth replied, "We haven't seen your Mr. Ashcroft, Mr. Kincaid. I have no idea where he is or what might have happened to him. I sincerely hope that he's all right, however."

Kincaid snorted contemptuously. "No offense, ma'am, but I don't believe you."

"You're quick to call a woman a liar, Mr. Kincaid. If you spoke that way to a man, there would probably be gunplay."

"Are you threatening us, Miss Crawford?"

"Just pointing out the fact that you're not much of a gentleman," Beth said coolly.

"Hell's bells!" Kincaid exploded. "My foreman is missing and probably dead! I don't have time to worry about being a gentleman!"

A new voice joined the conversation. "Take it easy, Pa." That was Harley Kincaid, Longarm knew. "You'll have a spell if you don't calm down."

"The only spells around here are the ones cast by that witch woman!" snapped Kincaid.

"Mr. Kincaid!" Beth said. "I'll thank you to keep a civil tongue in your head."

"Or else what, lady? You'll turn me into a pig or some such?"

Longarm frowned. He recalled reading some old Greek myth in which men had been turned into pigs by a witch, but he was a little surprised that Kincaid had read it, too. Or maybe the rancher's comment was just a coincidence. It didn't really matter.

"Pa—" Harley began again, only to have his father interrupt him.

"Damn it, I want to know where Jed is, and I want to know now!"

"If we see Mr. Ashcroft, we'll get word to you immediately," said Beth. "But in the meantime, I'll thank you to leave my ranch, Mr. Kincaid. I don't feel any obligation to be hospitable to someone as rude as you are!"

"Rude? Lady, you ain't seen rude yet!"

Longarm heard horses' hooves shuffling around.

"Come on, boys," Kincaid called. "We're riding into Salem Valley."

"I can't stop you," Beth said, and Longarm heard desperation edging into her voice, "but I really wish you wouldn't—"

"The hell with that!" barked Kincaid. "That's where Jed was headed, and that's where I'm going now!"

And if Bull Stennett and the rest of the outlaws were up there, Kincaid and his men might ride right into an ambush. They could easily be massacred.

Beth couldn't stop the rancher, but Longarm could.

A couple of strides put him at the door. He flung it open and stepped out of the cabin, fighting to maintain his balance as he did so. He didn't want Kincaid to know how badly he had been hurt.

Kincaid and half a dozen riders with him were turning their horses away from the cabin. Longarm shouted, "Hold it, you men!"

Martin Kincaid's eyes widened with surprise as he saw Longarm standing there shirtless in the cold Wyoming air, gripping a Winchester as if he were ready to use it. "Long!" he exclaimed. "What are you doing here?"

"Stopping you from making a bad mistake," replied Longarm.

Kincaid's eyes flicked from Longarm to the Crawford women and back again. He gave Longarm an ugly smile. "Reckon you happened onto a mighty nice deal for a drifter," he said. "A couple of pretty women, all alone . . ."

"Pa!" Harley yelped. "You shouldn't talk like that!"

Beth and Melinda were both blushing deeply. Longarm forced down the anger he felt and said, "Another day I might give you a whipping for that, Kincaid, but right now there ain't time. You can't go riding blind into Salem Valley."

"Why the hell not?" demanded Kincaid. "Who's going to stop us?"

"I am," Longarm said calmly, keeping the Winchester pointed in the rancher's general direction.

"Why would I let a no-account drifter tell me what to do?"

"Because that no-account drifter happens to be a deputy United States marshal."

Kincaid, Harley, and the other riders stared at him, thunderstruck. Longarm noticed from the corner of his eye that Beth and Melinda didn't seem nearly as surprised.

Well, of course not, he told himself. They had undressed him, after all, when they brought him back here to the cabin, and they had probably found the leather folder that contained his badge and bona fides tucked away inside his jacket.

Kincaid recovered from his surprise enough to say, "You're a lawman? The hell you say!"

"It's true," Longarm assured him. "Deputy Marshal Custis Long, working out of the Denver office."

"You got any proof of that?"

"Inside the cabin."

Beth spoke up. "It's true. Beth and I both saw his badge and identification papers."

Kincaid glowered at her and then at Longarm. "So you lied to me," he snapped. "I welcomed you into my house, and you lied to me."

Longarm gave a small shrug. "I'm up here working on a case, didn't figure it'd be a good thing to announce that. But I reckon I've got it figured out now, and that's why you can't go riding into Salem Valley."

Now all of them looked confused, including the two women. "What does Salem Valley have to do with your job, Mr. Long? Or should I call you Marshal Long?" Beth asked.

"It don't really matter, ma'am. As for Salem Valley, I reckon it's the hideout where a bunch of outlaws I'm chasing have holed up."

Kincaid's bushy eyebrows lifted again. "Outlaws?" he repeated.

"That's right," Longarm said with a nod. "The Bull

Stennett gang. You go blundering in there, and they're liable to bushwhack you and your men, Kincaid."

The rancher rubbed the beard stubble on his jaw. He had ridden out for the Circle Moon so abruptly this morning that he hadn't even shaved. He asked, "You're sure about that, Long?"

"Sure enough," said Longarm. He lowered the barrel of the Winchester slightly, sensing a chink in Kincaid's armor of outrage. "Tell you what. It's mighty cold out here to be standing around talking, especially for me. Why don't you and Harley and these ladies all come inside, and we'll hash it all out?" He nodded toward the barn. "The rest of your men can put their horses away. But look out for old Buck and his Greener. He's been sitting there in the hayloft ready to blast the lot of you ever since you rode in."

Longarm grinned as the old-timer poked his head out the opening in the barn wall that led into the hayloft and glared at him. Longarm had spotted the double barrels of Buck's shotgun as soon as he stepped out the door of the cabin.

Harley said, "I think we should listen to the marshal, Pa. We've always been law-abiding folks."

"Yeah, well . . ." Kincaid said reluctantly. "I want to see that badge, Long, before I'll really believe that you're a star packer."

"Come on inside, then," Longarm told him. He glanced at Beth and added, "I hope that's all right with you, ma'am."

She said icily, "I'm not in the habit of inviting people who threaten me into my house, but in this case I suppose I can make an exception." She lifted her chin and looked at Kincaid. "Please come in. There's coffee on the stove, and breakfast."

"Obliged," growled Kincaid as he swung down from the saddle. He didn't sound like he meant it.

Longarm didn't mind the insincerity. He just wanted to

get in out of the cold—he had goosebumps all over his torso by now—and find out the details of Jed Ashcroft's apparent disappearance. From the sound of it, the MK ramrod had been headed for Salem Valley, which didn't make a whole lot of sense to Longarm. He remembered how Ashcroft hadn't even liked talking in the bunkhouse about the so-called cursed valley.

When he had straightened that out, Longarm would likely have a proposal for Martin Kincaid. Longarm couldn't clean out that nest of outlaws by himself, but with Kincaid and the crew from the MK backing him up as an unofficial posse, that would be a different story. It would take some planning, though.

But with any luck, thought Longarm as he went inside with the others, before too much longer Bull Stennett and the rest of the outlaws would be either captured or killed, and his job here in Wyoming would be done.

The way it had been going, that couldn't happen soon enough to suit him.

13

"Jed didn't want to go, but he felt like it was his job," Martin Kincaid was saying a few minutes later as he sat at the table inside the cabin. He had a plate of food and a cup of coffee in front of him, like the others at the table. "When that bull broke out of its pen and its tracks led up here, Jed decided he had to come after it."

"He should've told somebody about it besides Horse Collar, though," added Harley. "He should've brought some of the hands with him."

Longarm sipped the steaming coffee and gratefully felt its bracing effect. "Ashcroft didn't like that valley," he commented. "Reckon he figured he shouldn't put anybody else at risk."

During the time that had passed since the near-showdown outside, Longarm had finished dressing. He still got dizzy if he moved too fast or too suddenly, but overall he felt stronger now.

Kincaid had explained how, two days earlier, Jed Ashcroft had discovered that the MK's best bull had busted down one side of its pen and disappeared. An experienced cowboy, Ashcroft had been able to follow the bull's tracks to the Circle Moon and then on to the wall of cliffs where the passage to Salem Valley was located. He'd lost the tracks on the rocky ground at the base of the cliffs. Returning to the MK, he had mentioned to the cook, Horse Collar Jones, that he planned to venture into Salem Valley the next day in search of the missing bull. Horse Collar had not realized until this morning that Ashcroft had gone alone.

And had not come back.

"I saw no sign of Mr. Ashcroft while I was checking our herd yesterday," Beth said to the small group gathered around the table. "And Melinda was here, keeping watch over Mr. Long, so she wouldn't have seen him, either."

"That's right," Melinda confirmed. "I was out of the cabin a few times during the day, but I didn't see any riders."

"How about that old-timer who works for you?" asked Kincaid.

Beth shook her head. "Buck doesn't ride horseback anymore, since his bones got so brittle. He stays close to the cabin and the barn and the corrals."

Harley said, "I'll bet Jed would steer clear of here, anyway, and go around to reach the cliffs."

"Why would he do that?" Beth asked coolly.

Harley suddenly looked embarrassed, as if he wished he had not brought up the subject. "Well . . ."

"Ashcroft figured you ladies for witches," Longarm said with a faint smile. "I suppose he didn't want you to know he was snooping around, for fear of what you might do to him."

Kincaid snorted. "I've known Jed Ashcroft for fifteen years. He ain't scared of man nor beast." The rancher frowned. "But I guess when it comes to spooks and haunts and such . . ."

"For God's sake," Beth burst out, "we're supposed to be witches, not ghosts!"

"It's all supernatural," Harley said.

Longarm steered the conversation back to the point by saying, "There's nothing supernatural about Bull Stennett and his gang, and they're the ones I think are holed up there in Salem Valley."

"You're sure of that?" Kincaid asked sharply.

Longarm shrugged. "No, I ain't sure. But I've been looking for 'em for a while, and this is the most likely place for a hideout I've found so far."

"It *would* make a good hideout," mused Kincaid. "Hard to find, only one way in or out, easy to defend . . . I've heard of this owlhoot called Stennett. He's supposed to be pretty smart."

"Nobody's caught him yet. That says something for him."

They had been eating as they talked. Finished now with his meal, Kincaid pushed away the empty plate and said, "All right, Long, I'll accept that you're a lawman. And if you're right about that valley being full of outlaws, poor Jed could've ridden in on them and got himself killed. But I have to find out, one way or the other."

Longarm nodded and said, "I know, but I plan to go with you."

"I don't know if that's a good idea," Beth put in. "You have a head injury, Mr. Long. I've heard that such things can be quite dangerous, and it's hard to tell just how badly you're really hurt."

"I know better'n anybody else how hard this old noggin of mine is," insisted Longarm. "I'll take it easy as much as I can—but I'm going."

Beth sighed. "I didn't think I'd be able to talk you out of it." She paused, then went on, "You know, Melinda and I have been living here for two years, and we've seen no sign of this outlaw gang you described, Marshal. If they're using Salem Valley as a hideout, wouldn't we have seen them coming and going?"

"Not if it was always in the middle of the night."

"What about tracks? Wouldn't they have left tracks that we would notice?"

Longarm shrugged. "Maybe, if you were looking for

them. But there's a lot of rocky ground around here, and maybe Stennett has his men brush out their tracks everywhere else."

Kincaid pushed back his chair from the table. "That's enough palaver," he declared. "I'm ridin' for the valley."

"Maybe we should get some more men from the ranch first, Pa," Harley said worriedly. "If we're going up against a bunch of desperadoes, we're liable to need more help."

Kincaid frowned, torn between caution and his natural impulsiveness. But he finally nodded, and Longarm knew Kincaid realized his son was right. "You ride back to the MK," he said to Harley, "and round up as many of the boys as you can. Just leave Horse Collar and a couple of men there to keep an eye on the ranch."

Eagerly, Harley got to his feet. "I'll go right now." He grabbed his hat from where he had hung it on the back of his chair and clapped it on his head as he hurried out of the cabin.

Longarm drank the rest of his coffee. "I'll run the show," he said to Kincaid as he set the empty cup on the table. "That means that what I say goes."

Kincaid bristled. "I ain't a lawman, Long. I don't take orders from you."

Longarm shook his head and said, "Whether you like it or not, I'm deputizing you and all your men, Kincaid, which means you *do* take orders. That's the only way I'll let you go with me."

Kincaid's eyes narrowed. "We're back to the question of how in Hades do you expect to stop us."

"You're a law-abiding man," Longarm said. "I'm counting on that to stop you."

"I've also got a top hand and an old friend who's disappeared. Would *you* worry about going by the book if Jed Ashcroft was your pard, Long?"

Longarm wished Kincaid hadn't asked him that question. Billy Vail likely could've cited chapter and verse on all the times Longarm had bent the rules. Sometimes he not only failed to go by the book, he forgot it even existed.

But he wasn't going to let Kincaid buffalo him. "That's the way it's going to be," he said harshly.

For a long moment, Kincaid made no response. Then the rancher said, "I'll cooperate, Marshal . . . as long as it doesn't put Jed's life in danger."

Longarm was convinced that Ashcroft was probably already dead, but he nodded anyway. "It's a deal," he said.

Harley Kincaid was back in less than two hours with another ten men. Counting Longarm, Harley, Kincaid, and all the ranch hands from the MK, nineteen riders started off from the Crawford cabin bound for the cliffs and the almost-hidden entrance to Salem Valley.

That was more than two to one odds in favor of the impromptu posse, Longarm told himself as he rode at the head of the group next to Martin Kincaid. More than enough to allow them to corral Bull Stennett and the rest of the outlaws.

But as he looked at the rocky cliffs rising before them, he had a bad feeling gnawing at his guts like a rabid weasel. Something wasn't right, but with the pounding that was going on inside his skull, he couldn't force his brain to tell him what it was.

As the group of riders drew closer to the cliffs, Kincaid said, "If this owlhoot Stennett is as smart as you say he is, Long, he might have a lookout planted somewhere up there."

"It'd surprise me if he didn't," agreed Longarm.

"Then we may be riding into an ambush."

Longarm nodded grimly. "It's possible." He looked over at Kincaid, who shrugged after a moment had passed. The message was clear. They would just have to do the best they could.

No shots rang out as the posse came closer and closer

to the cliffs, however. For some reason, that made Long-arm's uneasiness increase. A silence hung over the rugged landscape, broken only by the thudding of hooves. Rising darkly in the distance, Black Butte loomed over the cliffs.

Longarm could understand why some folks thought the valley was cursed. Even in daylight, an air of gloom cloaked the entrance to the place.

The riders reached the cliffs. Longarm led them straight to the gash in the earth that marked the trail to Salem Valley. They entered the passage, the hoofbeats of their mounts echoing hollowly and eerily against the sheer stone walls.

Martin Kincaid's voice was a harsh whisper as he said, "Don't look like they're waitin' for us after all."

Longarm shook his head. "I wouldn't count on that."

But as they followed the twisting, turning trail and pen-etrated farther and farther through the cliffs, Longarm was forced to admit that the rancher might be right. If Bull Stennett knew they were coming, he hadn't prepared a hot-lead welcome for them.

Maybe, by some miracle, they were going to catch the outlaws unaware of the threat closing in on them.

Longarm pulled his Winchester from its sheath and rode with the rifle across the saddle in front of him, ready for use. His eyes darted between the narrow passage up ahead and the tops of the cliffs far above. He was alert for any movement, any sort of warning sign that would tell him they were about to be bushwhacked.

Nothing.

"This just ain't right," he muttered. He had fully ex-pected that the posse might have to fight its way into Salem Valley.

Finally, after what seemed like an hour of following the passage, the end came in sight. Longarm's heart, al-ready slugging heavily in his chest, increased its pace even more, which likewise increased the pounding in his head. The last hundred yards of the passage leading to the opening into the valley was a straightaway. This was the last place Stennett and the other desperadoes could ambush the posse. . . .

Longarm put his horse into a run. Beside him, Martin Kincaid followed suit, and Harley and the rest of the men did likewise, trailing Longarm and Kincaid closely. Longarm was ready to snap the stock of the rifle to his shoulder and fire if anyone fired at them.

The posse reached the end of the passage and thundered out into the valley. Longarm immediately waved for them to spread out. Bunched together as they were of necessity, they made a hell of a target.

If anybody had been shooting, that is. Longarm hauled back on the reins, bringing the dun to an abrupt halt. He half-lifted the Winchester and looked around. A few yards away, Martin Kincaid was similarly poised for action.

But Salem Valley was as peaceful and quiet as the weekly meeting of a ladies' quilting society. Quieter than some, Longarm thought.

Kincaid looked over at him. "Where are the outlaws?" demanded the rancher.

"They could still be here somewhere," Longarm began. "This valley is a big place—"

He broke off as he heard the crackle of gunfire in the distance. With a cold horror blooming inside him like a flower on a grave, he wheeled the dun around and looked back the way they had come. The sound of the shooting was coming from beyond the cliffs that formed the barrier into Salem Valley.

The shots were coming from *outside*.

From the direction of the cabin where he had left Beth and Melinda Crawford alone except for the stove-up old puncher called Buck.

Longarm knew now what he had forgotten, and he prayed his oversight wasn't costing the women their lives.

14

With a harsh yell, Longarm kicked his mount into a run toward the passage through the cliffs. The faint popping of gunfire continued from the other side.

Even though it was less than a mile in a straight line to the other side of the cliffs, the sharp angles of the trail meant that Longarm and the other men would have to cover considerably more than that distance to reach the Crawford cabin. And they couldn't gallop through most of the passage, either, but would have to take it slow.

Longarm's jaw clenched tightly. He wished the dun could sprout wings and fly, so that he could simply soar over the cliffs and get where he wanted to go in a hurry.

But that was impossible, of course. All he could do was get to Beth and Melinda as quickly as possible, and if anything had happened to them, Longarm vowed that he would spend the rest of his life, if necessary, hunting down the men responsible for it.

As the posse entered the passage through the cliffs, something whipped past Longarm's head. A fraction of a second later, he heard the sharp crack of a rifle. The report echoed back and forth between the walls. More shots blasted, adding to the echoes.

Behind Longarm, one of the other riders screamed in

pain. Bullets sang around the heads of the possemen as Longarm yanked his horse to a halt and looked up at the rimrock. He spotted movement up there, flung his rifle to his shoulder, and fired.

He couldn't tell if he hit anything or not. The ambush continued. Longarm glanced around and saw that a couple of Kincaid's men were down, knocked out of their saddles by bushwhacker lead. He waved the group back toward the opening into the valley and shouted, "Get out of here! Move, damn it!"

Riders struggled to bring terrified horses under control. They raced for the relative safety of Salem Valley. Longarm and Kincaid brought up the rear, twisting in their saddles to snap shots toward the bushwhackers on the rimrock.

Suddenly, Longarm heard an explosion and then a low, rumbling sound behind them. He reined in, turned around, and saw a cloud of dust beginning to rise from deeper in the passage.

"Son of a bitch!" he bit out angrily through clenched teeth.

Martin Kincaid had stopped, too. He said, "That sounded like dynamite!"

"They blasted the walls," said Longarm bleakly. "The passage is probably closed now."

"But that means . . ."

"We're trapped in here," Longarm finished as the rancher's voice trailed off.

He had ridden right into the jaws of the trap Bull Stennett had laid for him, he thought bitterly. Even worse, he had led Kincaid and the other men into it with him. If they all died in this cursed valley, their lives would be on his head.

His aching head. He might not have been so careless if he had been able to think straight, he realized. But the clarity of thought that seemed to be returning to him now had come too late.

The gunfire had died away with the rumble of the blast that closed the passage. No doubt the riflemen were fleeing to rejoin the rest of the gang, confident that the posse was bottled up in Salem Valley. As the echoes died away, Longarm listened intently. He didn't hear any shooting from the direction of the Circle Moon, either. Whatever had been going on at the women's cabin, it was over now.

"Damn it," snapped Kincaid, "what are we going to do now?"

Harley rode up to his father and Longarm. "Isn't there some other way out of here?" he asked.

Longarm was starting to think about that himself. The glimmer of an idea had come to him. "There has to be," he said slowly as he rubbed his jaw. "Stennett and his men saw us coming and got out of here, but we didn't meet them in the passage. That means there has to be another exit."

"Well, then, we'd better find it," said Kincaid. "And fast, too."

Longarm nodded and turned to peer along the length of Salem Valley.

This was his first good look at it in daylight. While there was plenty of rugged, rocky ground that wouldn't be good for much of anything, there were also sizable patches of vegetation, especially along the narrow creek that meandered from side to side of the valley. Given the difficulty of moving cattle up here, Beth Crawford was right: it wouldn't be worthwhile for a rancher to do so.

But a band of outlaws could certainly hide here. Longarm put his horse into a walk and ordered the rest of the posse to spread out.

"Some of you head for the cliffs on both sides of the valley," he told the riders. "Look for anything that might indicate another way out of here."

The cowboys from the MK nodded their understanding and spurred away on the mission Longarm had given them. That left a group consisting of Longarm, Kincaid,

Harley, and a couple of punchers riding down the center of the valley.

"If we can find where Stennett and his men spent their time, maybe we can trail them from there to the other exit," Longarm mused, talking as much to himself as to his companions. He wanted to be careful to think everything through this time and not make the same sort of mistake that had landed them in this predicament.

Salem Valley was half a mile wide and perhaps three miles long. Longarm reckoned they had covered more than half the valley's length when they came to a dip in the landscape that hadn't been visible until they were nearly on top of it. He reined in at the top of the slope.

Down below was a small log cabin with a corral made of peeled poles beside it. Longarm knew he was looking at Bull Stennett's hideout at last. The irregularity in the terrain explained why he had not been able to spot a light when he first entered the valley several nights earlier. Even if a lamp had been burning inside the cabin that night, he wouldn't have been able to see it from where he'd stood at the mouth of the passage through the cliffs.

The outlaws' cabin looked deserted now. No smoke came from the stone chimney, and the corral was empty. Still, after everything that had happened, Longarm didn't fully trust appearances. He held the reins in his left hand and the Winchester in his right as he kneed the dun into motion again and started down the slope.

The other riders with him were ready for trouble, too. Longarm glanced at them and saw that Martin Kincaid's face was set stonily. Harley looked a little nervous, though. The young man had boasted of helping to fight Indians when he was eight years old, but in recent years this had been a fairly peaceful area. Going up against a band of outlaws led by a man as smart and ruthless as Bull Stennett had to make the boy a little edgy.

Longarm was confident that Harley would be all right,

though. The youngster hadn't panicked during the ambush.

Motioning silently for the MK punchers to circle the cabin, Longarm rode directly toward the rough dwelling. He watched the windows and was ready to fire at any movement he spotted. There was nothing to shoot at. The closer he came, the more confident Longarm was that the owlhoots were long gone.

He stepped down from his saddle, kicked the door open, and went through it in a rush. Kincaid was right behind him.

The cabin was empty, just as Longarm suspected. The outlaws had left behind a few empty cans and some other trash, but that was all. The ashes in the fireplace were barely warm, Longarm discovered as he knelt to check them. Stennett's gang had pulled out early this morning, probably as soon as they spotted the posse approaching the passage through the cliffs.

Longarm and Kincaid went outside. Longarm shook his head as Harley looked curiously at him. "They're gone," he said. "Just like I figured."

Harley pointed at the corral and said, "There are some tracks. Maybe we can follow them."

That was what Longarm was hoping. He and Kincaid mounted up again as the other two men rejoined them.

Longarm was a more than adequate tracker. He was able to follow the trail left by the outlaws when they abandoned the cabin. It led toward the western wall of the valley. Some of the cowboys from the MK were working their way along that wall, but Longarm wasn't going to wait for them to discover the gang's back door. With one eye on the ground, he rode toward the dark cliffs that hemmed in the valley.

The trail disappeared where it crossed an outcropping of rock that shouldered up out of the ground. Longarm cast back and forth along the stony stretch but was unable to find the tracks again. Still, he was confident they were going in the right direction. The trail had been pointing straight toward the western wall of the valley when it vanished.

Suddenly, doubts struck him. He had fouled up earlier, and his mistake had placed Beth and Melinda in danger. He already knew that Stennett was a tricky bastard. Maybe Stennett *wanted* him to follow those tracks. Maybe the outlaws had doubled back when they reached the rocky ground.

Longarm paused, rubbed his eyes, gave a little shake of his head. Kincaid reined in beside him and asked, "What's wrong, Marshal?"

"I . . . I ain't sure," Longarm said. He was used to charging ahead, hell-bent-for-leather, and most of the time, that was the right course of action. Now, the uncertainty that he felt was maddening. He had insisted on leading the posse, but he didn't know what to do. For one of the few times since he had pinned on the badge, he felt control of himself and of the situation slipping away from him.

He took a deep breath and stiffened his spine. He couldn't allow this to happen. The men with him were depending on him to get them out of this trap safely. Beth and Melinda were probably depending on him to come to their rescue, too . . . if they were still alive.

Longarm banished that thought from his head. Until he saw differently with his own eyes, he was going to believe that the women were alive and at least relatively safe. The only reason Stennett would have raided the Circle Moon was to grab Beth and Melinda as hostages, and for that he needed them alive.

"Marshal?" Kincaid prodded.

Longarm gave a determined nod. "We'll check out those cliffs along the western side of the valley." He heeled the dun into a trot.

Almost immediately, he felt better again. He rode toward the cliffs with the other men trailing him.

These rocky heights weren't as sheer as the ones that blocked the southern and northern ends of the valley, but they were much too steep for horses to climb. That meant there had to be another way out. Longarm and his companions came to the creek, which bubbled along merrily. Longarm's eyes tracked it to the edge of the valley, and he suddenly wondered where the stream came from.

A few minutes later, he knew. The creek emerged from a dark hole at the base of a bluff. The tunnel was barely wide enough for a man on horseback, and low enough so that he could have to stoop to ride into it. The horse would have to actually wade in the creek, too.

Kincaid brought his mount to a halt beside Longarm's. "Reckon that's where they went?" he asked.

"Only one way to find out," Longarm said. "The rest of you stay here."

And with that, he urged the reluctant horse into the tunnel.

15

Melinda Crawford gritted her teeth to keep from crying as she swayed back and forth in the saddle. Her wrists has been lashed to the saddle horn, and the rawhide strips used to bind them had been pulled cruelly tight. If she had to ride like this all day, her wrists would be rubbed raw and bloody by the time the group of riders stopped.

Melinda glanced over at her aunt. Beth's jaw was swollen and bruised where one of the outlaws had hit her, but her eyes were clear and glittered with anger.

These men didn't know what they had done by raiding the Circle Moon, thought Melinda. Not by a long shot.

There were seven of them, including their leader, the one called Bull. Bull Stennett, that was his name, Melinda recalled hearing Marshal Long say. The name fit him. Stennett was built like a bull with his thick neck, broad shoulders, and barrel chest. His jaw thrust out arrogantly, and his Stetson was jammed down on thick, curly black hair.

Stennett must have felt Melinda's eyes on him, because he hipped around in the saddle and grinned at her. She glared back at him, and he laughed.

"That's right, gal," he told her. "You keep that feisty attitude. It'll make tamin' you that much sweeter."

"Melinda." Beth spoke in a low, forceful voice. "Ignore him, Melinda."

"Yes, ma'am," the younger woman grated.

Stennett looked at Beth, and his expression grew even more lecherous. "And you, lady," he said, "you're goin' to be even more fun."

Beth stared off into the hazy distances of the basin to the west. After a moment, Stennett laughed again and turned back around in his saddle.

Melinda and her aunt exchanged a glance. Melinda took some comfort from the strength she saw in Beth's face. They were in a bad fix, true, but neither of them had given up hope.

Maybe Marshal Long would find them, Melinda thought. Stennett had seemed confident that the marshal and his makeshift posse were trapped in Salem Valley, maybe even dead, but Custis Long had struck Melinda as a stubborn man in the best sense of the word. The marshal wouldn't give up. It would take death to stop him.

Melinda let her mind wander back to that morning, when she had brazenly taken off her nightshirt in front of the marshal, even though she had suspected that he was awake. When they had locked eyes as she stood nude before him, she had felt the heat of desire growing in her belly. Melinda was not as innocent as she looked, and she would have enjoyed getting to know Marshal Long better. That was another reason to hate Bull Stennett, for ruining those plans Melinda had begun to make.

Beth and Melinda had been about to ride out and check the cattle in the pastures when Stennett and three other outlaws showed up. Melinda had known as soon as she saw them that something was wrong. She had realized that they weren't members of the posse, and since they were coming from the direction of Salem Valley, that meant they had to be some of the men Marshal Long was after. Outlaws and ruthless killers.

The two women had made a run for the cabin, and

when the raiders saw them fleeing, the men had whooped and drawn their guns and started firing. The commotion had drawn Buck out of the barn, and no matter how long she lived, Melinda knew she would never forget the horrible sight of what had happened next.

As the outlaws swarmed past the barn, a couple of them had triggered shots at Buck, who was trying to scramble back to cover. The slugs had caught the old man in the back and driven him through the open barn door, into the shadows inside. That was the last Melinda had seen of him, but she didn't see how he could have survived the shooting. She felt her eyes growing damp now as she thought about the old-timer.

The distraction Buck had provided had given the two women time to reach the cabin and get inside. The thick log walls were sturdy enough to stop most bullets. Melinda had slammed the shutters over the windows while Beth snatched rifles from the pegs where they hung on the wall and loaded them. Then, firing through chinks that had been put there for that purpose, they had tried to drive off the outlaws.

Stennett and his men were stubborn, though, and poured lead at the cabin. A few of the bullets found tiny openings and penetrated, ricocheting dangerously around the room. Beth stayed cool, trying to draw a bead on any outlaw who was foolish enough to show himself. Melinda drew strength and inspiration from her aunt's courage.

During a lull in the firing, they'd heard a distant explosion and a faint rumble following it. At the time, they'd had no idea what was going on. Later, after the women had been taken prisoner, Stennett had boasted of the trap he'd set for Marshal Long, Martin Kincaid, and the rest of the posse.

"Hated to give up what's been a good hideout for us," Stennett had said. "But if that lawman found it, it ain't no good to us no more. We'll just have to find us another one."

There was plenty of food and ammunition in the cabin, and even some water. Beth and Melinda might have been able to hold out for quite a while, but there were only two of them. They couldn't cover all the approaches to the cabin. Some of Stennett's men had been able to get close enough to throw flaming torches onto the roof, and that had been the end of it. When the choking smoke got too thick inside the cabin, they'd had to come out, and the owlhoots had grabbed them, knocking Beth around in the process.

Then they'd been put on their horses and tied into the saddles, and the outlaws had ridden out with their prisoners. Melinda had begged them to let her check on Buck, but Stennett and the others had just laughed at her. The old man was dead, they told her.

That had to be true. If Buck had still been alive, everything would have been different.

They had left Circle Moon range and were on Kincaid land now. In fact, thought Melinda, they probably weren't far from the ranch house. Maybe someone there would be able to help them.

But then she remembered how most of the MK punchers had been brought to the Circle Moon by Harley Kincaid to join the posse. It was entirely possible that no one was at the ranch house except the cook and a couple of men. They wouldn't be any match for Stennett's gang.

Melinda's heart sank. She didn't want to give up, but it was looking more and more as if it was going to take a miracle to help her and her aunt escape from these desperadoes.

Nick Larson had his eyes on the smoke curling into the sky to the north as he brought his buggy to a stop beside the barn. Something was on fire between the MK and Black Butte. The only ranch up that way was the Circle Moon, the small spread owned by Beth Crawford and her niece. Nick had seen the women in Greybull on occasion but didn't really know them.

He wasn't surprised that the MK appeared deserted. Someone down here probably had spotted the smoke, too, and everyone had gone off to see what was burning and if they could help. Martin Kincaid might not like Beth Crawford very much, but Nick had been out here on the frontier long enough to know that neighbors pitched in to help each other, even when there was no love lost between them.

He stepped down from the buggy and knotted the horse's reins around a post. "Hello?" he called into the barn.

To his surprise, a couple of men came ambling out a moment later. He recognized them both as punchers who rode for Martin Kincaid. One of the cowboys said, "It's that lawyer fella."

The other man asked, "What can we do for you, Larson?"

"Is Harley here?" Nick said. He knew he was risking Martin Kincaid's wrath by coming out here again, but he still hoped to be able to persuade the rancher to register his claim properly. Nick and Harley had been friends since college, and Nick didn't want to see the ranch that Harley should own one day snatched away from his friend.

"Naw, Harley and ever'body else have gone up to Salem Valley," replied the second puncher. He gestured toward the north, then looked again sharply in that direction. "What the hell!"

"Looks like the witch's house is on fire!" exclaimed the other cowboy. Nick realized they hadn't noticed the smoke until just now.

The two men turned to hurry toward the corral, clearly intending to saddle up and ride off to check out the fire. Nick stopped them by grabbing the arm of the smaller man.

"Why did Harley and the others go to Salem Valley?" he asked. He knew how the locals felt about that place. The whole idea of the valley being cursed seemed like silly superstition to Nick, but he knew that many of the cowboys believed in it.

"He said they were goin' to help some lawman roust out a bunch of outlaws," answered the cowboy. He jerked his arm loose. "Something must've gone damn wrong!"

That was certainly true, thought Nick. He didn't know anything about lawmen or outlaws, but it sounded to him as if Harley might be in serious trouble. He ought to go with the MK punchers, he decided.

Before he could untie the buggy horse, he heard the rapid pounding of hoofbeats. Thinking that perhaps Harley and the other men were returning, Nick turned toward the sound.

Instead of seeing his friend and the rest of the punchers from the MK, Nick saw a bunch of strangers galloping toward the barn. The hard-faced men had their guns drawn. Nick heard a shout of alarm from one of the MK cowboys and glanced back to see both of them reaching for their guns.

Shots began to slam through the air, and when Nick looked again at the newcomers, he saw smoke and flame geysering from the barrels of their weapons.

Instinctively, Nick flung himself toward the buggy. He carried a small pistol in the buggy for protection against wild animals, but he wasn't after the gun. He scrambled behind the vehicle, trying to find whatever cover he could. He heard bullets thudding ominously against the wall of the barn behind him.

The two cowboys returned the fire of the invaders, but they were outnumbered and too far away from any shelter. Nick watched in horror as bullets ripped into the two men. They crumpled into limp heaps on the ground, and blood began to pool around their bodies.

The strangers galloped up to the barn and trained their

guns on the buggy. "Come out from behind there, mister," one of the men ordered in a harsh voice. He was big and seemed to be the leader.

Nick raised his hands to shoulder lever and tried to keep them from trembling too much as he straightened from his crouch and stepped out from behind the buggy. He had never been more frightened in his life.

He saw to his shock that the raiders had two women with them. The women were prisoners, their hands bound to their saddle horns. Nick recognized them as Beth Crawford and her niece, Melinda. Beth's face was bruised and swollen, and both women looked frightened.

The leader of the killers glared at Nick and asked, "Who the hell are you?"

"N-Nicholas Larson," Nick managed to say shakily. "Attorney at l-law."

"A lawyer, eh? I reckon that means you're an important man. Good. Three hostages are better'n two, I suppose, even if one of 'em is a milk-faced townie like you, mister."

Hostages? Nick thought. He was a hostage? He swallowed a groan of dismay.

They had never taught him in law school how to be a hostage.

Or how to die, either.

16

The dun Longarm was riding hated the dark and hated the cold water splashing around its hocks. Longarm didn't much blame the horse.

The tall, rangy lawman had to bend over uncomfortably in order to ride through the tunnel. Every time he straightened up even a little, his head bumped the rocky ceiling. It was dank and chilly inside the tunnel, though the air was not quite as cold as it was outside. Being underground like this moderated the temperature somewhat.

When Longarm had ridden far enough so that the light from the tunnel entrance no longer reached him, he fished out a lucifer and snapped it into life with an iron-hard thumbnail. The darkness was so thick that it swallowed up the feeble glow from the match within a few yards. But that was enough light so that Longarm could make his way along the passage without having to worry too much about running into a wall or falling into a chasm.

The tunnel ran relatively straight, but it curved enough so that the tiny dot of light far behind him that marked the entrance was soon lost from view. Longarm pushed on, sensing the oppressive weight of countless tons of dirt and rock above him. He had never liked tunnels. He recalled being trapped in one down in New Mexico Territory on a previous case, and the only good thing about that had been the good-looking blond he'd had for company. And the fact that they had both made it out of there alive, of course.

The dun shied a little as the water grew deeper around its legs. "Sorry, old son," muttered Longarm. "We got to keep going."

The simple fact of the matter was that there was no room to turn around. The walls of the tunnel almost brushed Longarm's shoulders. This passageway was very much like the one through the cliffs at the southern end of the valley, except that it wasn't open at the top. Longarm had to keep going forward or try to make the horse back up all the way to the entrance. That would be a chore, he knew.

He let each match burn down as far as he could before dropping it and lighting another one. He had a couple dozen of the lucifers, but there was no telling how long this tunnel was.

Once, when he had just lit a fresh match and the flame was burning strongly, he stopped and watched it closely. The flame didn't waver, and that wasn't a good sign, he realized. It meant the air inside the tunnel wasn't moving at all, as it should have been, even if only a little, if the other end was open.

Maybe Stennett had rigged some sort of crude door at the far end, something that could be opened and closed to keep the tunnel hidden when the outlaws weren't using it. Longarm hoped that was right.

He found out fifteen minutes later that it wasn't.

Longarm didn't have to rein the dun to a halt. The horse stopped on its own as it came to an irregular wall of fallen rocks. Longarm sniffed the air, smelling dust and a faint whiff of burned powder. More dynamite had brought down the ceiling and closed this end of the tunnel, just as the explosion outside had blocked the other way out of Salem Valley.

Longarm bit back a curse as he stared at the solid mass of rock. A crew of miners with drills and pickaxes might be able to dig through the barrier, but Longarm knew he could not. Not with his bare hands, working by himself. Even if all the members of the posse pitched in, the quarters were too close for more than one or at the most two men to work at a time.

It would take them weeks to dig their way out, Longarm thought grimly.

But there was water in the valley and probably some wild game for food, so ultimately the men who were trapped there ought to survive.

That was a small relief, but not much of one. Longarm knew that by the time he and the others got out of the valley, Stennett and his men would be long gone. In that amount of time, they could be anywhere from Canada to Mexico, from the Barbary Coast to Boston.

Longarm had a bad feeling that Beth and Melinda Crawford had been taken prisoner by the gang. Stennett might keep them alive for a while, but Longarm knew the outlaws would probably tire of them and kill them eventually.

"Damn it!" he exclaimed as the match he was holding burned his fingers. He dropped the lucifer and sat there in the darkness for a moment after the tiny flame flickered out. There had to be some other way. . . .

But he was damned if he could see it. With a sigh, he said to the dun, "I know you probably hate backing up, old son, but there ain't nothing else we can do. Come on."

He tugged on the reins and started the horse moving backward. That was even slower than going forward through the tunnel had been.

After what seemed like an endless amount of time, Longarm looked over his shoulder and saw the tunnel entrance. He kept the dun backing up until finally they emerged into the open air again. Longarm blinked. Even though the day was somewhat overcast, it still seemed awfully bright to his eyes after all the time he'd just spent underground.

The other men were waiting for him, including the ones who had been futilely searching the other side of the valley for a way out. "What did you find?" Martin Kincaid asked anxiously.

Longarm took off his hat, surprised to find that he was sweating slightly. He wiped the sleeve of his jacket across his forehead, then said, "Stennett and his men must've gotten out that way, but the other end is blocked now. I reckon they blasted it just like they did the other way out."

Kincaid cursed sulfurously for a minute, then asked, "Can we dig our way out?"

"Eventually," said Longarm. "It's going to take a long time, though, because there's only room for one man, maybe two, at the end of the tunnel. Depends on how far the tunnel's collapsed, of course, but even if we work around the clock I reckon we're still looking at days before we get out of here."

"Who knows where Stennett will be by then?"

Longarm nodded grimly. "That's the problem, all right."

He tipped his head back and studied the steep walls of rock looming above them. He wondered if a man could climb them. It might be possible, even though there were stretches where Longarm couldn't see any footholds or handholds, no matter how hard he looked. And even if a man got to the top, could he work his way around to the southern end of the valley and get back to the Circle Moon?

He was going to have to give it a try, he realized. He couldn't just sit here in Stennett's trap, not knowing what had happened to Beth and Melinda.

"You fellas get started digging," he said. "I'm going to try to climb out."

Kincaid looked at him sharply. "You can't do that.

Hell, a mountain goat'd have trouble getting up those rocks."

"Don't have any choice," Longarm said with a shake of his head. "If I can get out, I can fetch help, maybe find the other end of that tunnel and start digging through from the outside. That'll get the rest of you out a lot quicker."

"Not if you fall and kill yourself," Kincaid pointed out.

"I don't intend to do that."

Harley spoke up for the first time since Longarm had come out of the tunnel. "Two men would stand a better chance," he said. "They could tie themselves together with rope, then if one man slipped, the other could catch him."

His father snorted. "Or get pulled down himself."

"I know a little about rock climbing," Harley insisted. "While I was in school back East, some of us went climbing a few times."

"They don't have any real mountains back east," Kincaid said contemptuously.

Longarm rubbed his jaw. "The boy may be right. If there were two fellas, they could help each other over the harder places."

"You've both gone loco," snapped Kincaid. "I won't allow it."

"I ain't one of your punchers, Kincaid," Longarm said. "In fact, I'm running this posse, remember?"

"You go ahead and break your damn-fool neck if you want to, Long. But Harley's my boy, and I say he ain't goin' with you!"

"I'm a grown man, Pa," said Harley, "and I'm going with the marshal."

Kincaid's face flushed a deep, angry red, and he probably would have continued arguing if Harley hadn't heeled his horse closer to the rock wall and taken his lasso loose from his saddle. "Give me your rope, too, Dave," he said to one of the MK punchers. "Marshal Long and I will use one rope for climbing and one to tie ourselves together."

"Blast it, boy—" Kincaid began.

Harley ignored him and took the rope from the other puncher. He swung down from his saddle and started walking along the rock face and studying it, looking for the best place to start the climb.

Even under the circumstances, Longarm had to smile a little to himself at the way the youngster was standing up to his father. Once this was all over, Kincaid would probably be proud of Harley for acting like this.

Unless, of course, Harley went and got himself killed.

Longarm put that thought out of his mind and dismounted to join the young man at the base of the cliff. Kincaid sat his horse nearby, fuming silently now.

Harley pointed. "Looks to me like we ought to be able to climb up along there," he said as he indicated the route he had chosen.

Longarm nodded and said, "We'll give it a try." In a lower voice, he asked, "You sure about this, Harley? I can go by myself."

Harley took a deep breath and blew it out. "I'll go, Marshal," he said. "We really will have a better chance if there's two of us."

Longarm thought so, too. He grinned at the youngster and clapped a hand on his shoulder. "Let's go."

The rest of the men gathered around to slap Harley on the back and wish him and Longarm good luck. Each of them tied one end of the rope around his chest, under his arms. Longarm carried the other rope coiled over his left shoulder.

Harley led off on the climb, finding handholds and footholds and hauling himself up. Longarm followed below him, occasionally pointing out where Harley might want to go next. He knew not to look down, but after a few minutes he estimated that they had climbed about fifteen feet.

The wall here was at least a hundred feet high, and the climbing was going to be harder the higher they got. Longarm cautioned himself not to get impatient. Slow and steady, that was the way to reach the top.

The rocks were cold and had thin patches of ice on them in places. Longarm's breath fogged in front of his face. Despite that he found himself growing warm inside the sheepskin jacket. It was too late to take it off now, he knew. He kept climbing, staying about five feet below Harley and a few feet to his left.

After what seemed like a long time, Harley paused. Longarm looked up, and the young man gestured at the stretch of rock just above them. "I can't see any places to catch hold," said Harley.

Neither did Longarm. He reached for the rope on his shoulder. "See that rock jutting out up yonder?" he asked.

"I . . . I think so," Harley replied.

"Reckon you can dab a loop on it from down here? If you don't think you can, I'll give it a try."

"I'll do it," Harley said decisively. "I'm higher." He turned and reached down for the lasso.

Longarm handed it to him and watched intently as Harley shook out the loop at the end. It shouldn't be too difficult a throw, thought Longarm, but the fact that Harley would be making the toss one-handed while clinging to the side of a cliff with the other hand made the odds worse.

"Careful," Longarm said.

"I can do it," Harley insisted, and Longarm wondered who he was trying to convince: Longarm . . . or himself.

Risking a glance below, Longarm saw that Martin Kincaid and most of the cowboys were still there watching. A couple of them were missing, though, and Longarm figured Kincaid had sent them into the tunnel to start digging. Kincaid still sat on horseback, his spine rigid.

"All right, here we go," Harley said, and as he gave the loop a couple of twirls over his head, he leaned out from the rock face to give himself a better angle on the throw.

That was when one of his boots slipped, and he suddenly plummeted backward and down, falling free toward Longarm.

17

Melinda was glad to get the rawhide thongs off her wrists, but she just traded one set of bindings for another as the outlaws hustled their prisoners into the parlor of the MK ranch house and tied them onto ladder-back chairs.

Stennett himself tied Beth, while one of the other men jerked Melinda's arms behind her and used a piece of cord to lash her wrists together. The chairs where they were seated faced each other. Melinda saw Stennett reach around from behind her aunt and cup Beth's breasts, squeezing them roughly through her shirt. The outlaw behind Melinda laughed, and she was afraid he was going to follow his leader's example.

A second later, her fear was confirmed as she felt the man's hard fingers dig into her breasts. He pawed them for a moment, still laughing harshly. Melinda's face burned with a mixture of rage and humiliation as she endured the coarse mauling.

Another of the outlaws shoved Nick Larson into the parlor. The lawyer's hands were tied together behind his back, but his legs were free. He was stumbling and off balance, though, and another push from his captor sent him sprawling on the thick Indian rug in front of the fireplace. He cried out as he landed painfully.

Melinda felt sorry for him. She didn't really know him, just enough to recognize him on the rare occasions when they crossed paths in town, but she knew he was an easterner and unaccustomed to the sort of rough treatment he was getting from Stennett's gang.

Of course, no one would ever get used to that sort of manhandling, no matter how long he lived on the frontier.

And how long they were all going to live was a good question, thought Melinda.

"Take a look around the place," Stennett ordered his men as he straightened from his pawing of Beth. "Could be those two punchers we already gunned down were the only ones here. Looked like most of Kincaid's crew was with that damned lawman when he started up to Salem Valley."

Melinda was afraid that was entirely possible. There might not be anyone else here on the MK to help her and Beth and Larson.

Beth spoke up, asking in a voice that betrayed not a single hint of fear, "What are you going to do?"

"Besides havin' us some fun with you two gals?" Stennett replied with a lecherous sneer. "I figured we'd load up on supplies and take whatever guns and ammunition and valuables we can find here. Then, after a few days, we'll drift northwest, up toward the Snake River country. We'll have to find us a good place to sit out the winter."

"A few days?" Melinda heard herself repeating. "You're going to stay here for a few days?"

Stennett swung toward her. "Why not, little lady? We got the place to ourselves. Kincaid and his boys won't be able to get out of that valley for a week or more, if they're even still alive. Could be that blast we used to close the trail finished them off, too."

Melinda didn't want to believe that. She had to cling to the thought that Marshal Long was alive and would come to rescue her and her aunt. And now the lawyer needed rescuing, too.

Tightly, Beth said, "You, sir, are a cold-blooded killer."

Stennett laughed. "Tell me something I don't know. I figure anybody dumb enough to get in my way deserves to die."

Beth's eyes narrowed. "What makes a man like you?" she asked. "What factors combine to turn what should have been a human being into a soulless animal?"

Stennett's mouth twisted, and he stepped closer to Beth. His hand came up and cracked savagely across her face, jerking her head to the side.

Melinda screamed, "No! Leave her alone!" She strained futilely against the cords that held her to the chair.

Stennett ignored her and pointed a finger at Beth. "You just keep your mouth shut, bitch. Whatever's in my past is my business, not yours." He was breathing heavily from anger. With a visible effort, he calmed himself and went on, "I called you a bitch, but you're really a witch, ain't you? Me and the boys stayed out of towns, pretty much, but we slipped into Greybull now and then to get a drink and bed the whores. We heard all about how there was a witch woman livin' up by Salem Valley and how most folks wouldn't go up there because of it. That's one reason we decided it might make a good hideout."

A tiny trickle of blood came from Beth's mouth where Stennett had struck her. She looked up at him defiantly and said, "I'm not a witch. If I were, I'd have turned you into a toad before now."

"Haw!" Stennett threw back his head and laughed. "I'd like to see you try it, lady!"

A sudden commotion from the door leading into the rest of the house made Stennett and the other outlaws turn sharply. One of the bandits came through the door, prodding another man at gunpoint. "Found this old bastard out back in the cook shack," the outlaw said.

Melinda recognized the long face and jug ears of the man known as Horse Collar Jones. The ranch cook glared around at the outlaws and demanded, "What're you fellers doin' here?"

"Taking over, old man," Stennett said. He stepped closer to Horse Collar and slipped his gun from its holster. For a horrible second, Melinda was afraid Stennett was going to kill the cook in cold blood, but instead the outlaw's arm went up and then lashed out, slashing the barrel of the Colt across Horse Collar's face. The cook grunted in pain and fell to his knees from the blow. Blood dripped into his eyes from the gash on his forehead opened up by the gun sight.

"Tie him up, too," ordered Stennett. "We might get tired of eatin' our own cooking before we leave."

"You can go to hell!" blazed Horse Collar. "I wouldn't cook up a big mess o' cow turds for you sons o' bitches!"

Stennett kicked him in the belly, then as Horse Collar doubled over in pain, Stennett kicked him again, this time in the head. Horse Collar sprawled out on the floor, knocked unconscious by the attack.

Stennett spat on the cook, then said, "Tie him up anyway. But if the old bastard don't learn to keep a civil tongue in his head, he may not live long enough to cook anything for us!"

The boss outlaw turned back to the other prisoners. "You've seen what'll happen to you if you don't cooperate," he went on. "Do as you're told and keep your traps shut, and you might just come through this alive."

Melinda stared down at the floor. She didn't believe a word of what Stennett was saying. She had seen with her own eyes the brutality and ruthlessness of the man. For now, the prisoners had a little value as hostages. When that was over—or when Stennett simply tired of keeping them alive—he would kill all of them. Melinda was sure of it.

She squeezed her eyes shut. She wished she could make it all go away. She wished there was some truth to the silly rumors of witchcraft that had gone around the basin.

If she'd had any supernatural powers at her disposal, she would have used them before now.

But she wouldn't turn any of the outlaws into toads, as her aunt had suggested.

No, if she had the power, thought Melinda, she would send each and every one of them screaming into the very pits of hell. . . .

Nick Larson licked his lips nervously. The muscles in his arms ached miserably because of the way his wrists had been pulled behind his back and tied, and his shoulder hurt even worse from landing on it when he fell. If he hadn't landed on the thick rug, he might have broken a bone. As it was, his hands had gone numb from being tied so tightly, and he didn't think he could get up to save his life.

Or anyone else's life, for that matter. He hoped that the Crawford women weren't counting on him to get loose and save them from the outlaws. He had never been in a fight in his life, let alone one with the sort of man who would kill without compunction.

Nick looked at the women and saw that the younger one—Melinda, was that her name?—was watching him. He slanted his eyes away, unwilling to meet her gaze. He didn't want to see the fear and desperation in those blue eyes.

Under other circumstances, they would have been pretty blue eyes, he found himself thinking. Beautiful, even. Melinda herself was a very attractive young woman, and her aunt was lovely, too. The thought of the two women being subjected to whatever cruel indignities those outlaws could come up with . . . It made Nick clench his teeth in shame that he couldn't help them.

The four prisoners were alone in the parlor now except for one man who had been left to stand guard over them. Stennett and the rest of the outlaws were out prowling around the ranch headquarters, looking for something to steal, no doubt.

Nick willed his muscles to move and tugged against the bonds around his wrists. They didn't give, but Nick wondered if he might be able to work some slack into them, given enough time. One good thing about his hands being numb was that he couldn't feel his skin being rubbed raw and bloody. . . .

What was he thinking? He closed his eyes and ducked his head, breathing rapidly and shallowly. Trying to escape would just get him killed more quickly. Of the four captives, he was the least useful to the outlaws. Horse Collar could cook, and the women . . . well, he knew how they would use the women.

Someone let out a snore.

Nick looked up in surprise. The sentry had tipped his chair back so that it was leaned against a wall, and his head was down on his chest. The outlaw had fallen asleep. He snored again, loudly.

Nick wasn't the only one who had noticed. He heard Melinda Crawford hiss, "Mr. Larson!"

Nick swallowed hard and looked at her. She inclined her head toward the sleeping guard, then jerked it several times as if to urge Nick to crawl in that direction.

He shook his head helplessly. What could he do? His hands were tied behind his back, and even if they weren't, he was no match for an outlaw.

Nick looked at Beth. She nodded emphatically, encouraging him to action just as her niece was doing. Nick was glad Horse Collar Jones was still unconscious, or else the cook would probably be trying to persuade Nick to commit suicide, too.

Against his will, Nick's eyes returned to the guard. They narrowed as he spotted the bone handle of a knife sticking up from the top of one of the man's boots. Nick suddenly wondered if it would be possible to slip that knife out of the boot without waking its owner. If he could, then he might be able to cut his bonds and make a grab for the gun holstered on the outlaw's hip. The revolver was right there for the taking.

But surely it would be impossible for his deadened fingers to manipulate the blade so deftly that he could cut himself free. Even if he could get hold of the knife, he would probably just slash his wrists and bleed to death before he could free himself.

On the other hand, the outlaws were going to kill him sooner or later, anyway. Nick was sure of that.

He looked at Beth and Melinda again, saw the silent pleading in their eyes. He told himself that he was crazy to even be considering such a risk.

Then, biting back a groan of effort, he began wriggling around and trying to pull himself up onto his knees. If he could get that far, he could crawl across the parlor to the guard and at least make a try for the knife.

After all, he thought bleakly, they could only kill him once.

18

As Harley fell with a terrified yell, Longarm lunged to the side, away from the plummeting young man. He was sure that from the ground it looked as if he were simply trying to get out of Harley's way, and to tell the truth that was part of it. Longarm couldn't save either of them if Harley knocked him off the rock face, too.

Longarm wrapped his arms around a bump of rock and dug in the toes of his boots as hard as he could. He held on for dear life as he felt the sudden jerk and strain on the rope tied around his chest. Harley's weight almost pulled him down as it hit the other end of the rope.

But Longarm was able to hang on, finding strength in desperation. He felt Harley swinging on the rope and called out to him. "Harley! Grab on to something! Harley!"

If Harley had been knocked unconscious when the rope caught and slammed him against the cliff, then they were both probably doomed. Longarm couldn't release his grip in order to pull Harley up, and he could only hang on for so long a time before exhaustion forced him to let go.

Down below, Martin Kincaid and the other men were shouting up at the two climbers. Longarm could hear them but didn't understand what they were saying. The pounding of blood in his head drowned them out.

"Mr. Long!"

Longarm heard that faint cry and knew it came from Harley. The youngster wasn't out cold, then, and that was good.

"Hang on, Mr. Long!"

Suddenly, Longarm felt the horrible weight pressing on his chest ease. The rope went slack. He drew in a deep breath, grateful for the relief. He might have passed out if the ordeal had gone on for much longer.

Turning his head and craning his neck, Longarm looked back over his shoulder. He saw Harley climbing toward him. The young man appeared to be a little shaky, but that came as no surprise. Falling like that was enough to unnerve anybody.

"That's it," Longarm called encouragement to him. "Slow and easy, old son."

Longarm saw that the rope Harley had been trying to throw was still tangled around his arms. That was a lucky break, too. If they had lost that second rope, they wouldn't be able to keep on climbing.

Gradually, Harley drew even with Longarm and paused about six feet to his right. "I . . . I'm sorry, Mr. Long," he panted. "I thought I could do it. . . ."

"Don't worry about it," Longarm told him. "I'm just glad I was able to grab on to something in time."

"Me, too," said Harley fervently.

"See if you can hand me that rope," Longarm suggested. "I used to be pretty good with a lasso when I was cowboying for a living."

Harley untangled himself from the rope and tossed one end of it to Longarm. Longarm caught it and pulled the rest of the rope over to him. He straightened it out, shook out a loop, and braced himself for the throw. After twirling the loop a couple of times to get the feel of it, he made the toss.

It fell short.

Sighing and gritting his teeth, Longarm gathered in the rope and got ready to try again. This time, when the lasso sailed through the air, the loop settled down cleanly over the outcropping of rock that was Longarm's target.

"You did it!" enthused Harley.

Longarm pulled the loop tight, then tugged hard on the rope. It seemed to be caught securely, and he knew it would hold his weight as long as it didn't slip off the rock.

"Get some good holds," he advised Harley, "and let me know when you're ready. I'm going up."

Harley dug in with his fingers and toes as much as possible, then nodded to Longarm. "All right, Marshal."

Longarm got a solid grip on the rope, then let himself sway backward slightly. The rope held. He began walking up the rock face, pulling himself along hand over hand on the rope. It was a harrowing few moments as he crossed the area where there were no handholds or footholds. Then, as he reached a more irregular stretch of cliff, he was able to dig in with his toes and take some of the strain off his arms. He sagged toward the face, settled himself into some secure holds, and let go of the rope. His muscles quivered a little as he rested.

"Mr. Long?" Harley called up to him anxiously.

Longarm took a deep breath and replied, "It's all right. Grab the rope and come on up, Harley. Just let me get set first in case you slip."

"I won't slip," vowed Harley, and this time he was right. He walked up the cliff the way he had seen Longarm do it, and within a few minutes he was beside the lawman again. Both of them were pale and breathing hard, and Longarm decreed that they would rest for a short while before continuing the climb. That was all right with Harley.

When they were ready to go again, Longarm loosened the rope from the outcropping, pulled it up, coiled it, and slipped it over his shoulder again. He and Harley resumed the climb.

Twice more during the next hour and a half, they had to use the rope to pull themselves up and over sections of the cliff where there was no other way to ascend it. Those climbs were as nerve-wracking as the first one, but they made it with no trouble and no more falls. The top of the cliff, which had seemed impossibly high when they started out at the bottom, was coming closer and closer now. Longarm was beginning to think they might just make it, then he immediately berated himself for allowing such hopefulness to enter his brain. He didn't want to jinx things.

There was no jinx. Fifteen minutes later, Longarm firmly gripped the edge of the rimrock and pulled himself up and over it, rolling in relief onto his back. Harley came over the top right after him and sprawled beside him. Longarm didn't know about the youngster, but his own muscles were trembling and he was breathing hard, as if he had just run a long race and couldn't get enough air into his lungs.

"Did you say you . . . climbed rocks for fun . . . when you were in school?" Longarm gasped out after several minutes.

Harley replied, "Yeah, but . . . never like that. That was tough." He didn't seem to be quite as winded as Longarm was. Youth was nothing if not resilient.

A few more minutes went by, then Longarm sat up. He leaned closer to the rim, so that he could look over the edge and down into Salem Valley. Just as he thought he would, he saw Martin Kincaid and the other men waiting anxiously below, peering up at the top of the cliff.

Longarm took off his hat and waved it back and forth a couple of times so that Kincaid would know they were all right. Kincaid cupped his hands around his mouth and shouted, "What do we do now?"

"Wait," Longarm shouted in reply. "We'll get you out of there soon as we can."

He clambered to his feet. Harley was already up looking around.

Longarm surveyed the terrain around them, too, as he untied the rope that bound them together. It was mighty rugged up here on the rimrock, he thought, but he could see paths where he and Harley could move south through the spires and knobs of rock.

"Mr. Long, I just thought of something," Harley said. "Will we have to climb down the other side?"

Longarm grinned tiredly. "Could be. We won't know until we get there."

Together they set off, making their way carefully over the rough, rocky ground. After a few minutes, Harley glanced over his shoulder and said, "I hate leaving Pa and the others back there."

"Don't worry too much about them," Longarm assured him. "Even if it takes a couple of weeks to get them out of there, they'll be all right. A mite hungry, maybe, depending on how slim the pickings are when it comes to game and plants they can eat, but they won't starve."

"Winter sometimes comes on fast up here," said Harley with a frown.

"I know, but they have that cabin to hole up in," Longarm said.

As if to tease them about the upcoming change of seasons, a few flakes of snow floated down from the leaden sky. It had been doing that off and on for several days, snowing infrequently and just enough to put a light dusting of white in isolated spots. Sooner or later, though, the sky would open up and dump several feet of the stuff everywhere.

The wind up here cut like a knife, and the fact that Longarm and Harley had been sweating from their exertions only made it worse. Longarm turned up the collar of his coat and tugged his hat down on his head. He wondered how long it would take them to walk to the far side of the rimrock.

Although they couldn't see the sun, the growling of his stomach told Longarm when it was midday. They trudged on, sometimes forced to clamber into and out of small gullies that cut across their course. Longarm hoped he was heading in the right direction. If he'd gotten turned around somehow and was walking away from the Circle Moon, he and Harley might wind up wandering in this wilderness of stone for days.

Finally, though, after several hours, they came to a sheer drop-off that extended as far as they could see in both directions. Longarm thought he recognized the cliffs as the ones that ran along the northern edge of the Crawford spread.

Harley agreed. "This is it," he said excitedly. "I recognize that range down there. The ladies' cabin isn't more than a mile east of here."

Longarm nodded. "Remember that question you asked me a few hours ago?"

"What question?"

"About having to climb back down when we got to the other side. Looks to me like the answer is yep, we sure will."

Harley chuckled. "Going down has to be easier than going up."

He was right. He and Longarm knotted both lassos together and tied one end firmly around a rock. The other end of the rope reached to within a dozen feet of the ground. They went down the rope one at a time, Longarm first. When he came to the end, he hung full-length and dropped the remaining five and a half feet to the ground, landing nimbly for a man of his size. He stepped back, took off his hat, and used it to wave Harley on down.

When Harley was on the ground, too, the youngster heaved a sigh of relief. He asked, "What do we do with the ropes?"

"Leave them there in case we have to use them to climb back up," suggested Longarm. "I'm hoping that ain't the case, though. I'd like to find that other end of that tunnel and open it up so your pa and the rest can come out that way. First, though, we'd better get over to the Crawford cabin."

"Why?" asked Harley.

"Maybe there'll be a couple of horses there. If we can round up some mounts, you can light a shuck for Greybull and fetch us some help." Longarm's jaw tightened. "I want to find out what happened to those women, too. From the sound of all the shooting earlier, they put up quite a fight."

Harley nodded and looked a little ashamed. "Yeah, I'd almost forgotten about that. I hope they're all right." He hesitated, then added, "I never did really think Miss Beth was a witch."

"Looks to me like they just happened to homestead the wrong place," said Longarm. "At least, it was the wrong place after Stennett and his bunch decided to move in."

They started walking again, ignoring the weariness that they both felt. Longarm let Harley take the lead, since the young cowboy knew the country hereabouts better than he did, and Harley's earlier statement about the Crawford cabin being close by proved to be true. The two men came within sight of it less than twenty minutes later.

"Hold on," Longarm said. "We'd better study a mite on the situation, just in case some of those owlhoots are still here."

He didn't really think that any of Stennett's gang would have stayed behind at the Circle Moon, but he couldn't rule out the possibility. He and Harley crouched behind the cover of some fallen pine trees for several minutes, watching the cabin, the barn, and the corral. Nothing appeared to be moving anywhere around the place.

But the cabin had been heavily damaged by fire, Longarm noted grimly. The roof was almost completely destroyed, while the walls were badly charred but still standing. It reminded him of settlers' cabins he had seen after Indian raids. The men who had done this were white, but they were every bit as savage as any bunch of Comanches or Apaches.

"All right," Longarm said in a low voice. "Whatever happened here, it's over now. Let's go see if we can find us some horses."

He knew they would have to look inside the burned cabin, and he was dreading that. If they found the bodies of Beth and Melinda Crawford, there was no place Bull Stennett could hide from him, thought Longarm. No place on earth.

Longarm drew his Colt as they approached the barn and motioned for Harley to do likewise. Harley slipped his gun from its holster. He was pale but seemed steady enough.

The door of the barn was open. Longarm paused just before he reached it, then swung around quickly and went through the opening, Colt leveled in front of him.

He froze as he found himself looking into the twin muzzles of a double-barreled shotgun, which stared back at him like black, soulless eyes.

19

Hardly daring to breathe, Melinda watched as Nick Larson edged closer and closer to the sleeping outlaw. When Nick was about five feet away, the man suddenly snorted and shifted in his chair. Nick froze.

The outlaw's eyes never opened, and after a horrible moment of uncertainty, he began snoring again. Nick closed his eyes for a moment, and Melinda wondered if he was offering up a prayer of thanksgiving or trying to muster the nerve to continue his attempt to reach the outlaw's knife. Or maybe both.

Nick swallowed hard, opened his eyes, and started creeping toward the guard again. Melinda and her aunt exchanged a tense glance as Nick drew closer to the sleeping man. Finally Nick was close enough to turn his back to the guard and use the hands tied behind his back to reach for the handle of the knife.

The front door of the ranch house banged open, and Bull Stennett strode into the room. He stopped short when he saw what Nick was doing and exclaimed, "What the hell!"

In a flash, Stennett was across the room, his fist lashing out at the lawyer. Stennett's knobby knuckles crashed against Nick's jaw and sent him sprawling on the floor.

Melinda screamed as Stennett jerked his gun from its holster and stood over Nick, cursing furiously. The boss outlaw eared back the hammer of his gun, and Melinda knew she was about to see Nick murdered in cold blood.

The man who had been left on guard had been awakened by the commotion. He jumped up from his chair and said hurriedly, "Honest, Bull, I didn't mean to nod off—"

Stennett whipped around, reversing the gun in his hand as he did so, and smashed the butt of the weapon across the face of the guard. The man fell, knocked to the floor by the unexpected blow. He lay there and whimpered in agony as he clutched his shattered jaw.

"I ought to put a bullet in your worthless carcass, Carlson," Stennett bellowed. "Be glad you're still alive."

The attack on the guard seemed to have taken some of the white-hot rage out of Stennett, but when he turned back toward Nick Larson, Melinda was still afraid he would shoot the helpless lawyer. Instead, Stennett holstered his gun.

Then he stepped forward and kicked Nick in the belly, just as he had kicked Horse Collar Jones. Nick doubled up in pain as much as he could with his hands tied behind his back, and although he retched, nothing came up.

"I ought to kill you, mister, but I won't," said Stennett. He grunted. "To tell you the truth, I didn't think you had the balls to try something like that, a townie like you. But if you try anything else funny, I'll put a bullet through your head. Got it?"

Nick didn't reply, and after a moment Stennett prodded him hard with the toe of his boot. "I asked if you got it, mister."

"I . . . I got it," Nick gasped out.

Stennett wheeled toward the two female prisoners. "Don't think I don't know who put this stupid bastard up to it," he said. "You two probably batted your eyes at him until he was ready to do almost anything."

In a low voice, Beth said, "Your brutality is amazing."

Stennett stepped closer to her, and Melinda wished her aunt had kept silent. "You talk too much, witch woman," Stennett said. "Why don't you do something useful with that mouth of yours?"

His fingers went to the buttons of his trousers.

Melinda closed her eyes in horror, thinking that she couldn't bring herself to watch what Beth was about to be forced to endure. The injured guard was still moaning thickly through his broken jaw, Nick Larson was still making small, ugly sounds, and all of it seemed even more heightened, more hellish to Melinda. She was beginning to wish she and Beth had stayed in the burning cabin and gotten it over with there, in the place that had been their home.

The door opened again, and a voice called excitedly, "Riders comin', Bull!"

Melinda's eyes snapped open. Stennett was still a couple of feet from Beth and hadn't finished opening his trousers. Melinda quivered with relief as the bandit chief fastened the buttons and strode toward the door.

Sooner or later, unless someone intervened and rescued them, she and her aunt would be attacked by the outlaws, Melinda knew. But any interruption that postponed that fate was more than welcome.

Stennett went outside, but he was back a minute later with two of the other outlaws. He said to his companions, "Take Carlson and that lawyer out back and keep them quiet."

One of the men helped the guard with the broken jaw to his feet and led him out of the room. The other one bent over, grabbed Nick Larson under the arms, and dragged him out.

Stennett jerked a knife from a sheath on his left hip and stalked toward Beth. For one awful moment, Melinda thought Stennett was about to stab her aunt, and Beth must have thought the same thing. Her face turned white with fear.

Then Stennett stepped behind Beth's chair and used the knife to cut the bonds around her wrists. "Stand up," he grunted. "I got a job for you."

"Not the same sort of task you were about to impose on me, I hope," murmured Beth as she came to her feet, pulled her arms in front of her, and began to massage her wrists where they had been tied.

Melinda silently willed her aunt to stop baiting Stennett. The outlaw's face tightened in anger, just as Melinda feared it would, but this time he was able to control himself.

"We'll talk some more later about that mouth of yours," growled Stennett. "For now, I want you to go outside and use it to tell those cowboys who are riding up to move on."

"Who are they?"

Stennett shook his head. "I don't know. Look like grubline riders, maybe. All I know is, I want 'em gone."

"And why should I help you?" Beth asked coolly.

Stennett drew his gun as he stepped over beside Melinda. He put the barrel of the Colt to her head, and she had never felt anything colder than that ring of metal as it pressed against her skin.

"Because if you don't, I'll blow this little bitch's brains out."

"Leave her alone," Beth snapped. "I'll do as you say."

"You'd damned well better, if you want this girl to be alive ten minutes from now."

Melinda had no doubt Stennett meant every word of the threat. Her life was hanging by a slender thread, one that could break at any second. The slightest pressure on the trigger of Stennett's gun would result in her death.

"Please," said Beth worriedly, "Be careful."

"You're the one who better be careful," Stennett told her. "Now get out there."

"But . . . but what do I tell them?"

"Anything, as long as you get rid of them. Tell 'em

you're the queen of the ranch if you want."

"All right," Beth said. "Just don't hurt my niece."

Stennett pressed harder on the gun barrel. "Go on."

Beth swallowed hard and then moved toward the door.

Melinda had never been so afraid in her life. This day had been nothing but a series of terrors, each worse than the one before. Now, with Stennett standing so close beside her with a gun to her head, she thought she might pass out.

She would have welcomed unconsciousness at that moment. At least if she was out cold, she wouldn't know it when the outlaw pulled the trigger and ended her life.

Maybe it wouldn't come to that, she told herself as she closed her eyes. Maybe her aunt would be able to convince the visitors—whoever they were—to leave.

Grub-line riders. That was what Stennett had said they looked like. Marshal Long had pretended to a man like that when he first came to their cabin. Maybe the men who were riding up to the MK ranch house right now were a whole posse of U.S. marshals. . . .

Beth had left the door ajar slightly when she went out, so Melinda could hear as hoofbeats pounded up to the house and then stopped. In a voice that was strong and confident, Beth said, "Hello, gentlemen. What can I do for you?" Melinda wondered how her aunt managed to sound that calm. She was thankful that Beth had such reserves of strength.

"Howdy, ma'am," said a man's voice. "We're looking for Mr. Kincaid."

"I'm afraid he's not here at the ranch right now," Beth said. "Did you have business with him?"

"Well, sort of. The boys and me, we were hopin' we might be able to hire on for the winter." The man paused, then went on, "From the looks of things around here, you're a mite short of cowboys."

Beth laughed. "I'm sorry, but the ranch has a full crew

right now, all we'll need until the spring roundup. They're just busy at the moment."

"Is that so?" A subtle change entered the man's voice. "So you're here by yourself, ma'am?"

"That's right," Beth replied. "So I'd be grateful if you gentlemen would ride on."

"And just who would you be, ma'am?"

Melinda could almost see the defiant lift if her aunt's chin as Beth replied stiffly, "I am Mrs. Kincaid."

It was an outrageous lie, of course, made even more so by the animosity between the MK and the Circle Moon. But these strangers wouldn't know that.

Or would they? The spokesman went on, "Now, that's funny. I don't recollect hearin' any talk over at Greybull about old man Kincaid bein' married."

"Well, he is, and I'm his wife," Beth said stubbornly, stuck now with the masquerade she had started. "My husband and the rest of the men will be back any minute, and I think it would be best if you and your friends were gone, sir."

"A polite woman. I like that."

It was so quiet in the house that Melinda could hear the faint creak of saddle leather, and she guessed that the man was dismounting.

"You'd better get back on your horse," Beth said angrily, confirming Melinda's guess. "You men are not welcome here—"

"You ain't even goin' to offer us something to eat, and water and grain for our hosses? We been ridin' a long way." The spokesman's voice was closer and louder now. Melinda wondered how many of the men there were.

"Under other circumstances, perhaps I would," Beth began, "but since you've been so rude—"

She broke off with a gasp as the cowboy said, "Lady, you ain't seen rude yet."

Beth's back hit the door and knocked it open as she struggled in the grip of the intruder. Through the opening,

Melinda saw the man holding her aunt's arms, and several other men were crowding onto the porch behind them.

"The hell with this," Melinda heard Stennett mutter. She expected him to kill her at any second, but the gun went away from her head and she almost fainted with relief.

"Hey!" Stennett yelled at the struggling couple in the doorway.

The cowboy looked up in surprise, and his eyes widened as he saw the outlaw and the young woman tied into a chair.

"You ain't hornin' in on this, you stupid bastard," Stennett told the stranger.

With a curse, the man shoved Beth away and grabbed for his gun. Stennett's Colt was already drawn and ready, however, and before the stranger could do more than touch the butt of his weapon, Stennett fired. Melinda saw the round black hole appear in the man's forehead, and the next instant the slug exploded out the back of the cowboy's skull in a spray of blood, gray matter, and bone fragments. He fell over backward, dead before he hit the porch.

The other men were shouting in confusion and trying to pull their guns, but the outlaws, no doubt well hidden where they could cover the porch, opened fire on them. Beth crawled frantically farther inside the house as rifle bullets raked the porch. The cowboys died where they stood, riddled by the barrage. They thumped to the ground, landing in lifeless, bloody heaps that Melinda could see through the open door.

She squeezed her eyes shut, unwilling to watch anymore.

The shooting probably lasted only a few seconds, though it seemed to go on much longer. Finally it stopped, and silence descended over the ranch house. Melinda opened her eyes again, saw Stennett holster his gun and bend over her aunt. He gripped Beth's arm and hauled her to her feet.

"You hurt?" he asked.

The question seemed to surprise Beth. "N-no, I don't think so," she said.

"Good. Go sit down, and don't move while I clean up this mess." He took hold of the legs of the man he had shot, who was lying half in and half out of the room. Stennett rolled the corpse completely onto the porch. "There."

Beth sank down in the chair where she had been bound. On the porch, Stennett gave orders to his men, telling them to find a ravine or some other convenient place to dump the bodies of the slain cowboys. "Put their horses in the barn," he continued.

He came inside and closed the door. "Damn fools," he said, apparently talking to himself as much as to the two women. "They could've ridden on and lived. You never should've told them you were alone, witch woman. Men like that, they ain't much better'n animals."

Beth looked up at him, still half stunned. "You killed them all," she said hollowly.

"Don't waste your time feelin' sorry for them," snapped Stennett. "They would've had their fun with you, then killed you, more than likely, before stealin' everything they could get their hands on. Might've even burned down the place just for spite."

"And just how are they different from you?" Beth asked.

"Biggest difference of all." Stennett grinned. "They're dead, and I ain't."

20

"Don't move," growled the old man called Buck as he aimed the shotgun at Longarm's face, "or I'll blow your damned head off!"

Longarm's Colt was leveled. "I could say the same thing to you, old son," he said. "Why don't you put that Greener down, and I'll holster this hogleg of mine, and we can talk about it?"

"Ain't nothin' to talk about," said Buck. "I don't trust . . ."

With that, his rheumy eyes rolled up in their sockets and the barrels of the shotgun sagged toward the ground as he passed out. Longarm had already seen the big bloodstains on the old man's shirt and hadn't figured that Buck could stay on his feet for long, so he was ready. His left hand shot out, grabbed the barrels of the scattergun, and shoved them aside just in case Buck's finger accidentally jerked the twin triggers.

As Buck fell, Longarm wrenched the weapon out of his hands. "Come on in, Harley," he said as he set the shotgun aside and went to one knee beside Buck.

The young man stepped into the barn and asked anxiously, "What's wrong with him?"

"Looks like he's been shot a couple of times, probably

in the back." Buck had fallen forward, so Longarm could see the bullet holes and the bloodstains on the back of the old man's shirt. The stains were smaller than the ones on the front, indicating that the holes in the front of Buck's torso were larger exit wounds. There were two wounds in front and two in back, so Longarm knew the slugs had gone on through and Buck wasn't carrying any lead inside him.

For whatever that was worth, considering that he had already lost enough blood to kill a normal man.

Longarm felt of the old-timer's stringy throat, looking for a pulse. When he found one, it was surprisingly strong. "See if there's a cot in the tack room," Longarm told Harley. "Since he's lived this long, maybe we can patch him up."

Harley ducked into the small room at the side of the barn's entrance and came back out a second later to report, "Yeah, there's a bunk in there. Looks like that's where he sleeps."

Longarm finally holstered his Colt. "Give me a hand with him."

Together, they carefully lifted Buck and carried him into the tack room, where they just as gingerly placed him on the bunk, positioning him on his left side.

Longarm began ripping away the blood-soaked shirt. "Look around and see if you can find a bottle of whiskey anywhere," he told Harley. "That'll do to clean these bullet holes as well as anything else we're liable to find out here."

Harley poked around the tack room while Longarm finished baring the old man's torso. A moment later, Harley found a brown bottle with a cork in it while he was digging inside an old trunk. He handed it to Longarm and asked, "Will this do?"

Longarm worked the cork out of the neck of the bottle and sniffed the contents. He made a face. "Smells like home brew, and mighty rank stuff at that. But at least it'll have alcohol in it. How about a clean shirt?"

Harley took one from the trunk.

"Cut me five good-sized pieces from it," instructed Longarm, "then start cutting the rest of it into strips about two inches wide." Harley fished a Barlow knife from his pocket and followed the orders.

Longarm took the first of the larger pieces Harley cut from the shirt and soaked it with the rotgut whiskey from the bottle. He began swabbing away the dried blood around Buck's wounds. When he was satisfied, he took the bottle itself and dribbled some of the fiery stuff into each of the bullet holes.

Buck hadn't moved or made a sound since passing out, but as the whiskey soaked into raw flesh, he shifted a little on the cot and let out a groan. His eyelids flickered, but he didn't regain consciousness.

Longarm sprinkled whiskey on one of the larger pieces of clean cloth, pressed it to one of the wounds, and told Harley to hold it in place while he bound it there with some of the strips the younger man had cut from the shirt. He bandaged each of the bullet holes in turn, then finally straightened from the bunk and took a small swig of the whiskey that was left in the bottle. "Damn!" he exclaimed. "That stuff's even more potent than I thought it was."

"Then it ought to be good for the old man, right?" asked Harley.

Longarm held up the bottle and regarded it. "If he's been drinking this panther piss regular-like, his insides are probably completely pickled. No wonder a couple of bullets couldn't kill him."

"You think he'll live?"

"We've done about all we can for him right now," Longarm said with a sigh. "He's lost too much blood and is too weak to put him in a wagon and take him to town, even if he does need to see a regular sawbones."

"I could ride to Greybull and bring the doctor out here."

"That's what you'll have to do. And bring the sheriff and every able-bodied man he can deputize back with you when you come."

"There are some horses in the stalls. I'll look for a couple of saddles," said Harley.

He left the tack room. Longarm pulled the room's single rickety chair over by the bunk and sat down to think. Buck's bullet-riddled state was proof enough for him that Bull Stennett's gang had been here. It would have been nice if the old man had been able to tell him, though, what had happened to Beth and Melinda. Longarm still hadn't looked in that burned-out cabin, and he supposed he ought to stop postponing that grisly task.

Suddenly, Buck shifted and moaned again, and as he tried to roll onto his back, Longarm held his shoulder and stopped him. "Rest easy, old son," said Longarm. "We've patched you up, and you're going to be fine."

Buck's eyelids fluttered again, and after a moment they came all the way open. "Y-you," he gasped. "The . . . lawman."

"That's right," Longarm told him.

"Knew I should've killed you . . . that first night."

Longarm frowned and leaned forward. "What do you mean by that?"

"Up yonder . . . on the trail to . . . Salem Valley."

Longarm's eyes widened in surprise. "That was *you* who shot me?"

"If'n I had my . . . scattergun . . .'stead of that old Walker Colt . . . I'd have got you for sure."

Longarm lifted a hand and touched the bandage that was still wrapped around his own forehead. "Well, if it's any consolation to you, Buck, it still hurts like hell where you creased me. Why in the world did you want to bushwhack me, anyway?"

"Knew you was . . . up to no good."

"I'm a federal lawman," Longarm said.

"Didn't know that . . . then . . . but it don't make no . . . never mind. You and your . . . damned posse." Buck took a deep breath and winced as the tight bandages pulled

136

slightly on his wounds. "If you hadn't come here . . . those gals'd still be . . ."

"Still be what?" asked Longarm, dreading the answer he might hear. *Still be alive?* Was that what Buck was trying to say?

"Still be here," Buck said.

Longarm felt his pulse quicken. "You mean Stennett and his bunch took Miss Beth and Miss Melinda with them?"

Buck gave a weak nod. "I tried to . . . get into the barn . . . and get my hands on my shotgun . . . when those bastards rode in. . . . They gunned me down . . . must've figgered I was dead. . . . I crawled deeper into the barn . . . where they wouldn't see me . . . tried to find my gun . . . I saw 'em set fire to the cabin. . . . When Beth and Melinda come out . . . those outlaws grabbed 'em. . . ."

Buck let out a long, rattling breath, and for a second Longarm thought the old man had gone beyond the great divide. But Buck's narrow chest continued to rise and fall, and after a moment he was able to go on.

"They put the gals on hosses . . . and rode off with 'em. Reckon I must've . . . passed out then. . . . Came to later and felt a mite stronger . . . so I managed to get up and get my Greener. Figgered to . . . saddle a hoss and go after 'em. . . . That's when you and the younker . . . showed up."

"Where did Stennett and his men take the women?" asked Longarm.

Slowly, Buck shook his head. "Don't . . . rightly know. But they rode off . . . headed south . . . toward the Kincaid spread."

Longarm didn't know if Stennett would have recognized Martin Kincaid and the riders from the MK or not, but it was possible. If Stennett thought most of the ranch's crew was trapped inside Salem Valley or dead from the avalanche that had closed the passage, he might believe it was safe to hole up at the MK for a while. There was at least a chance of that.

Harley came in while Longarm was pondering the situation. "I've saddled a couple of horses," the young man said. "We can head for Greybull any time you're ready, Marshal."

Longarm shook his head. "I'm not going to Greybull. You're going to have to handle that chore on your own, Harley."

Harley frowned. "Then what are you going to do, Mr. Long? Do you plan to stay here with the old man?"

Buck took offense at Harley's tone. "Old man . . . is it?" he said as he tried to push himself up on an elbow. "I can still whip . . . a dozen young scalawags . . . like you, boy."

Longarm put a hand on Buck's shoulder again and said, "Take it easy. I don't like leaving you here alone, Buck, but I reckon I'd better head for the MK."

"Why?" asked Harley.

Longarm hesitated for a second, then decided he had to tell the youngster the truth. "Because Stennett and his men may be holed up there, and they've likely got the women with them as prisoners."

Surprise and worry appeared on Harley's open, honest face. "But there's nobody on the ranch except Horse Collar and a couple of punchers. They couldn't defend the place."

Longarm nodded. "I know. That's why I think Stennett may be there."

Harley put his hand on the butt of his gun and said grimly, "You'll have to go to Greybull to fetch help, Marshal. It's my job to see to the MK."

Longarm stood up and went over to face Harley squarely. "You ain't listening, old son. *I'm* going to the ranch, and *you're* lighting a shuck for town. Dealing with outlaws is my job, not yours."

"You think I'm too much of a kid to handle Stennett and his bunch?" Harley asked angrily.

"I ain't sure a troop of cavalry could handle that gang," said Longarm. "Stennett's maybe the worst, but they've all still got the bark on. I'm just hoping maybe I can sneak in and get those two ladies out of there before any harm comes to them."

Harley paled. "Even outlaws wouldn't dare hurt a woman. They wouldn't be safe anywhere west of the Mississippi if they did."

"It's comforting to think that a code like that exists," said Longarm, "and maybe for most folks, even the bad ones, it does. But an hombre like Stennett don't care about any rules, written or unwritten. He'd just as soon kill those women as blink, if it suited him."

From the bunk, Buck groaned. "I should've stopped 'em," he said miserably. "I should've forgot about the gun and dealt with 'em the old way."

Longarm wasn't sure what he meant by that, and there wasn't time to worry about it now. The sooner he got to the MK, the better.

"The only chance Beth and Melinda have is for me to grab them away from Stennett," Longarm went on as he looked intently at Harley. "And the only chance to round up the gang is if you bring back plenty of help from town. How about it, Harley?"

The young man frowned darkly, shifted his feet, and grimaced. But then he nodded and said, "I reckon you're right, Mr. Long. I'll ride to Greybull, and I'll get back as fast as I can with all the help I can muster." He glanced at the wounded man on the cot. "And a doctor for the old-timer here."

"There you go again with that old-timer shit," muttered Buck, but now he was beginning to sound sleepy.

Longarm clapped a hand on Harley's shoulder. "Be careful," he said. "I could be wrong about where Stennett and the rest of those owlhoots headed."

"Do you really think the ladies are still alive?"

"They'd damned well better be," said Longarm, "or Bull Stennett's going to wish he'd turned himself in and died at the end of a hangman's rope."

21

Nick Larson slowly recovered from the savage attack that had left him huddled on the floor of the parlor in the ranch house. Another of the outlaws had been ordered by Stennett to stand guard, and after seeing what had happened to the unfortunate Carlson, this man wasn't just about to go to sleep on the job. Every time Nick glanced up, the hard-faced desperado was watching him intently, as if waiting for Nick to make another escape attempt.

Not likely, thought Nick. He was no hero. His earlier, clumsy attempt to free himself and the women was proof enough of that.

He just wished Beth Crawford and her niece would stop looking at him with hope in their eyes. Surely they had seen how helpless he was.

Beth was tied into her chair again, but Stennett hadn't returned to further terrorize her or Melinda. The boss outlaw had retreated into Martin Kincaid's office, probably to go through the rancher's desk looking for money. Nick knew that Kincaid also had a small safe, but Stennett wouldn't be able to open it without the combination. Unless, of course, he had some dynamite left over and blew the door off.

Finally, Nick felt strong enough to try to sit up again.

He rolled onto his side and awkwardly pulled himself upright. That made him extremely dizzy for a moment, and he had to close his eyes while his head settled down. He moaned.

"Mr. Larson? Are you all right?"

That was Melinda Crawford's voice asking the question. Nick forced his eyes open and looked at the young woman. With an effort, he summoned up a faint smile and nodded.

"Better not get any fancy ideas, mister," warned the outlaw who had been left on guard in the parlor. "I ain't goin' to make the same mistake Carlson did. You try anything, and I'll ventilate you, sure as hell."

Beth said, "The man whom Mr. Stennett struck with his gun, will he be all right?"

The guard glanced at her. "You mean Carlson? His jaw's broke, but I reckon he'll live. He ain't goin' to be eatin' solid food for a while, though."

Nick swallowed. His mouth was dry and had an awful taste in it, but he managed to say, "Why do you ride with a man like Stennett? You saw what he did to Carlson." Trying to drive a small wedge between Stennett and the rest of the gang might not do any good, but it couldn't hurt, either.

The guard laughed. "Carlson ain't rode with us long enough to know that you don't foul up when Bull gives you a job. Reckon he knows it now, though. Bull don't put up with mistakes. That's why we're all still alive." The outlaw grew more serious. "Best shut your mouth, mister. I ain't got time to talk to you."

Which meant that he was afraid of what Stennett might do if he came in and found the guard talking to the prisoners, thought Nick. Bull Stennett ruled this gang with an iron fist, through fear and intimidation.

But everyone had to have a weakness, a chink in his armor. Nick had learned that in law school. Part of being able to argue a case successfully in court was the ability to find that weakness in opposing counsel and exploit it.

He wasn't in court now, Nick reminded himself, and he wasn't appearing before a regular judge. Bull Stennett was judge, jury, . . . and executioner.

Longarm reined in and leaned forward in the saddle. Earlier, on his way to the Kincaid ranch, he had heard gunfire in the distance, coming for the direction he was headed. The shooting hadn't lasted long, and when the brief flurry of gunfire was over, silence had descended over the rugged Wyoming landscape. Ever since then, Longarm had stopped from time to time and listened intently, but there had been no more shots.

Longarm had no idea what the fracas had been about, but his instincts told him that Bull Stennett was involved somehow. He was more convinced than ever that Stennett had ridden down to the MK after leaving the Crawford spread. The shooting had surely been unlucky for someone, but Longarm was looking at it as an indication that Stennett wasn't too far ahead of him.

He was loaded for bear . . . or Bull, as the case might be. He had his Colt on his left hip in its cross-draw rig, an old Henry rifle he'd found in the barn was snugged under his right leg in a saddle sheath, and he was holding Buck's Greener across the saddle in front of him. Even with all that armament, he was still going to be heavily outnumbered and outgunned when he caught up to the outlaws.

Which meant he would have to find some way to gradually even the odds. A grim smile plucked at Longarm's mouth under the sweeping mustache. He had been taught how to read sign by a wizened Arapaho elder, and he had learned something of how the Indians fought from the old man, too. Indians were experts at whittling down the odds when they were dealing with a superior force. In order to do that, a man had to be able to move silently, to strike fast when he needed to, and to kill without hesitation.

142

Longarm figured he could manage.

More snowflakes floated down around him, and then the wind kicked up, whipping the flakes around like grains of sand. Longarm rode for another half hour, then stopped as he caught sight of a thin spiral of smoke in the air ahead of him. The smoke was hard to see because the sky was so gray. Longarm watched it for a few seconds, figuring it probably came from the chimney at the MK ranch house. The smoke was just about in the right place for that.

Someone had lit a fire in the big stone fireplace, he told himself. Not surprising, since the temperature seemed to be dropping. And there was nothing about smoke from a chimney that would warn a visitor anything was wrong. In fact, it would look downright normal, and that was what Stennett would want right now.

Longarm pushed on, swinging his mount to the east so he could approach the ranch from that direction. If he remembered correctly, the pine forests were thicker over there in the foothills and would give him more cover.

By late afternoon, he felt that he was close to the ranch headquarters. Stennett only had half a dozen men, so there likely wouldn't be any outriders patrolling this far from the house. There would certainly be guards close by the place, though.

Longarm reined in, dismounted, and tied the horse's reins around a sapling. He slid the Henry from its sheath and carried it in his left hand. His right was wrapped around the grip of the shotgun. With an easy grace that was unusual in such a big man, Longarm cat-footed through the woods toward the ranch.

He stopped and crouched behind some brush, parting the branches with the twin barrels of the Greener so that he could see through the gap. The ranch house was a couple hundred yards away. The fact that it sat up on a knoll by itself was going to be a problem, thought Longarm. He was confident that he would be able to sneak up on the barns and the corrals, but the house itself was a different story. A distraction might be required if he was going to be able to get inside.

After several minutes of keen-eyed studying, Longarm had located a couple of the outlaws, the proof he needed that Stennett had moved his hideout here to the MK for the time being. One of the men was in the main barn, crouched just inside the partially open door of the hayloft, smoking. The glowing coal at the end of the quirly was what gave him away, a tiny red dot inside the shadows of the barn. It was a good hiding place for a bushwhacker, because no one could go up the slope toward the front of the ranch house without presenting an excellent target to the rifleman waiting in the hayloft.

The other guard Longarm spotted was at the back corner of the ranch house itself. He couldn't see any of the outlaw's body, but he saw about six inches of the barrel of a Winchester protruding around the corner.

There was probably at least one more man posted somewhere around the house, Longarm decided. But the man in the hayloft might be the only one in the barn. That made him the logical place to start.

Staying low so that the underbrush would hide him, Longarm began circling the barn. When he was fairly close to the back of the structure, he emerged from the brush in a crouch and ran toward the barn. He had to risk being out in the open for a few seconds; there was no other way to get inside.

No one shot at him or raised an alarm. With his heart slugging heavily in his chest, Longarm reached the barn and flattened himself against the rear wall. After pausing for a moment to catch his breath, he began edging toward the double doors. They were both closed, but they were fastened with a simple latch. When Longarm reached it, he carefully set the shotgun on the ground, then lifted the latch.

The doors were heavy, and he grunted quietly as he

eased the right-hand one open about a foot. The hinges were well oiled—he could thank Martin Kincaid for that, Longarm thought—and didn't make any noise. Again, no one shot at him, so he pulled the door back another foot. Now he could slip through. He picked up the shotgun and stepped into the barn.

The late-afternoon overcast meant that the interior of the barn was cloaked in thick shadows, but at least Longarm's eyes didn't have to adjust much, as they would have if the sun had been shining brightly outside. He left the rear door open behind him and moved soundlessly deeper into the barn.

Quickly, he spotted the ladder that led up to the hayloft. He set both the Henry rifle and the shotgun on the hard-packed dirt floor. He didn't want to alert the outlaws in the house, so he had to take care of this guard quietly. He began looking around for a means to do so.

Longarm's eyes fell on a pitchfork hung on a wall hook. That would be appropriate, he thought, considering that the guard was in the hayloft. Carefully, Longarm lifted the fork from the hook and carried it to the ladder.

He could only use one hand, since the other was occupied with the pitchfork. That made climbing awkward, but he managed. Slowly, quietly, Longarm climbed the ladder. After what seemed like a longer time than it really was, his head emerged from the open trapdoor in the hayloft.

The outlaw who was posted up here sat about twenty feet to his right, his back toward Longarm, peering out at the ranch house. The planks of the loft were covered with a layer of dust and loose hay, so Longarm was able to lay the pitchfork down without making any noise. He started to climb out through the trapdoor.

None of the rungs of the ladder had creaked so far, so Longarm was surprised when the top one let out a loud creak as he put his foot on it. By now he was in the loft, but he wasn't close enough to the guard to strike without warning. As the man heard the noise, he turned quickly, bringing up the rifle in his hands.

Longarm could have reached for the Colt, but he still didn't want any shooting if he could avoid it. So he did the only other thing he could. He snatched up the pitchfork and heaved it at the guard like an Indian lance.

In his surprise, the guard hesitated just enough to allow the pitchfork to fly across the loft and hit him in the right shoulder. He sagged backward with a grunt of pain as two of the tines dug deeply into his flesh. The rifle fell from his hands and landed on the floor with a clatter, but it didn't go off.

For a second, Longarm thought the outlaw was going to tumble backward through the opening behind him. But then he caught himself with his left hand. He staggered to his feet as Longarm rushed him. Grabbing the pitchfork with his other hand, he jerked the tines out of his shoulder.

Longarm ducked as the outlaw jabbed the handle of the pitchfork at his face. He reached up and grabbed the handle. The outlaw was wearing a six-shooter, of course, and Longarm was glad he hadn't thought to pull the gun and let off a warning shot. Longarm kept the man occupied by trying to wrench the pitchfork away from him.

The two men struggled over the deadly implement in the grim silence that Longarm wanted. The outlaw tried to knee him in the groin, but Longarm twisted aside at the last instant and took the blow on his thigh. Longarm's head pounded. A man whose skull had been creased by a bullet only a few days earlier ought to still be in bed resting, not engaging in a life-and-death struggle with a ruthless owlhoot. But Longarm had no choice. He had to win this fight if he wanted to have a chance to save Beth and Melinda.

Longarm slammed his left fist into the guard's wounded shoulder. The outlaw paled and yelped in pain. His grip on the pitchfork loosened enough so that Longarm was able to yank it free. He jabbed the tines toward the out-

146

law's face, forcing the man to duck under the curved, razor-sharp points.

The outlaw launched himself forward, tackling Longarm around the waist. Both of them went down, sprawling in the dust and loose hay of the loft. Longarm still had hold of the pitchfork. He swung its wooden handle, cracking it across the outlaw's upper arm. The outlaw cursed and finally thought to reach for his gun, but his muscles didn't want to obey him. He fumbled awkwardly for the weapon, wasting a couple of valuable seconds that let Longarm roll away from him. Longarm came up on his knees and jabbed with the fork again.

This time one of the tines caught the outlaw in the wrist of his gun hand, penetrating easily so that Longarm felt the steel grate on bone. One of the other tines raked the man deeply on the hip, just above his gun belt. He cried out in pain, and Longarm hoped the yell wasn't loud enough to have been heard in the ranch house up on the knoll. Longarm yanked the pitchfork to the side, taking the outlaw's impaled gun arm with it. He drove the fork down, slamming the tines into the floor of the loft and pinning the man's wrist.

Longarm surged up and launched a kick, the toe of his boot catching the outlaw under the chin. The man's head was driven back sharply, and Longarm heard a crack like a tree limb breaking. The outlaw's body jerked once and then lay still. A small pool of blood began to form around his wrist, but it stopped spreading as the outlaw's heart ceased beating. Longarm's kick had broken his neck.

Breathing hard, Longarm dropped to a knee and checked for a pulse anyway. He didn't find one. The outlaw was dead.

One down, Longarm thought grimly.

22

Longarm pulled the pitchfork out of the planks—and the outlaw's wrist—then rolled the dead man over to the side of the loft and used the fork for the more prosaic task of tossing a pile of hay over the corpse. He also scattered more loose hay over the bloodstains.

If any of the other outlaws came looking for the dead man, they might not find him right away. All Longarm wanted was a little time to figure out his next move.

He knelt where he could look out the hayloft door at the ranch house, staying far enough back in the shadows so that no one in the house could get a clear look at him. The fight in the loft seemed to have gone unnoticed. The outlaws inside the house must be occupied with other things.

Longarm hoped that didn't include molesting the Crawford women.

He wondered if his best bet would be to wait until another outlaw came out to relieve the guard in the barn. Then Longarm could jump that man and dispose of him.

But there was no telling how long that would take, and he didn't like the idea of leaving Beth and Melinda in there with the rest of the gang any longer than he had to. He studied the terrain around the knoll. A frontal approach was out, and he didn't think there was enough cover on either side to let him get close enough to reach the house unseen. That left the back, and he knew there was a guard posted there.

Well, nobody had said it would be easy, Longarm told himself. He climbed down out of the loft, picked up the Henry and the shotgun, and left the way he had come in, hurrying back into the woods to the place he had tied the horse.

The animal was cropping patiently at a few tufts of grass that hadn't been killed yet by the change of season. Longarm mounted up and rode back into the foothills to the east of the ranch headquarters, keeping one ear cocked for a commotion that would tell him the body of the dead outlaw had been discovered.

He didn't hear anything, and once he was out of earshot, all he could do was hope that his luck would hold. He circled the ranch at a distance of at least half a mile before angling toward it again.

It would be dark soon. If he waited until nightfall, he would have a better chance of reaching the house, he decided. That meant Beth and Melinda would have to take their chances for a longer time, but it couldn't be helped. When Longarm found a good place to leave the horse, he swung down from the saddle again and tied the reins to a bush. Taking the rifle and the shotgun with him as before, he approached the rear of the knoll where the big house sat.

The closest cover was a small clump of pine trees. Longarm eased himself into a crouch behind a thick trunk and studied what he could see of the house. The slope cut off part of his view, and the light was getting bad, but after a few moments he was able to make out the shape of a man's hat near the corner of the house. That would be the guard whose rifle he had seen earlier from the front of the house.

As soon as it was good and dark, thought Longarm, he

would try to reach that guard and put him out of action. Then, if he could come up with some sort of distraction to draw Stennett and the rest of the gang out of the house, he could slip inside, locate Beth and Melinda, and set them free.

That was the plan, anyway.

And like so many plans, Longarm realized a moment later, there were things that could go wrong with it. Gunfire suddenly broke out from the front of the house.

Longarm bit back a curse. It would have been nice to be able to wait until dark. . . .

But he came up onto his feet and broke into a run, dashing to the bottom of the slope and starting up it toward the house, where shots continued to pop.

Melinda was grateful for the heat that came from the fireplace. The parlor had grown quite cold before Stennett came back in and ordered the guard to kindle a blaze. Now the warmth had spread through the room.

Stennett seemed to be in a good mood. He had a canvas bag full of money that he'd found in Martin Kincaid's desk. The safe in Kincaid's office had defeated him for the time being, but he planned to use dynamite to blow it open before the gang left the ranch house for good.

"The blast might start a fire," Stennett explained to one of his men, "so we'll wait until we're ready to ride out."

"You figure to torch the place anyway, don't you, Bull?" the outlaw had asked.

Stennett had nodded. "Sure. Best way to cover up evidence, ain't it?"

He had glanced at Beth and Melinda as he said it, and a chill had gone through Melinda that no warmth from the fireplace could chase away. Stennett planned to leave their bodies in the house when he rode away from the MK. They would be consumed in the inferno the outlaws would leave behind.

Now Stennett was sitting in one of the big, overstuffed

chairs near the fire, taking an occasional pull from a bottle of whiskey he had found. He had the canvas bag in his lap and was going through the money, seemingly enjoying the simple act of rubbing it together between his fingers. Melinda couldn't help but wonder about the same question her aunt had voiced earlier: what was it that turned a man into a killing, stealing machine like Stennett?

She would never know, she sensed. Not that it was important anyway. The outlaw was like a force of nature, destroying everything in his path just as a cyclone did.

One of the other outlaws hurried in from outside. "Somebody's comin', Bull," he reported.

Stennett looked up sharply from his chair. "What? Not again."

The other man shook his head. "It ain't like those cowboys who rode up in the open. This is just one fella, and he's tryin' to sneak up on us. Leon spotted him a minute ago, down by the barn."

"Travis is up in the loft," Stennett said confidently. "He can take care of anybody who tries to get up the hill to the house."

"Mebbeso, but he ain't took a shot so far."

Stennett frowned. "Maybe our visitor's already taken care of Travis. If he did, then he must be pretty good." Stennett came to his feet. He glanced at the guard. "Stay here, Dawson," he ordered, then said to the other man, "Let's go. We'll have a warm welcome waiting for whoever's out there."

Maybe it was Marshal Long, thought Melinda. She felt a surge of fear for the lawman, or whoever it was trying to slip up on the house. He was headed right into an ambush and didn't know it.

If only there was some way to warn him. . . .

Beth spoke up, saying, "Mr. Dawson, I . . . I hate to ask, but . . . I have to pay a visit to the privy."

The guard came a step or two closer to the women and put his hand on the butt of his gun as he shook his head.

"Sorry, lady," he said. "I got my orders. You ain't goin' nowhere."

"But . . . but I simply *must*." Beth's face was red with embarrassment, but Melinda wasn't sure the emotion was genuine. The timing of the request hinted to Melinda that maybe her aunt was up to something. Maybe Beth wanted to warn whoever was out there in the dusk, too.

"You'll have to ask Bull when he comes back—" Dawson's face suddenly showed understanding. He sneered at Beth and went on, "This is some sort o' trick, ain't it? You think somebody's tryin' to help you, and you want to let the bastard know that Bull's onto him." Dawson shook his head again and drew his gun. "You can just forget about that, lady."

He was concentrating on Beth and ignoring Melinda, and that was his mistake. Melinda saw her opportunity, realized that it was a desperate, slender chance, and seized it anyway. Her legs weren't tied to the chair, so she lifted her right one and kicked out at Dawson's gun hand, the heel of her boot catching him solidly on the wrist.

Dawson yelled in surprise and pain as the revolver sailed out of his hand and flew through the air to land in the fireplace. "Son of a bitch!" exclaimed the outlaw as he ignored the pain in his wrist and scrambled toward the flames, intent on recovering his gun before it was too late.

He didn't have time to snatch the weapon out of the fire. The cartridges in the cylinder began to explode from the heat, the sound of the shots echoing loudly up the chimney and from the stone walls of the fireplace itself.

Dawson spun around with a snarl and backhanded Melinda as he shouted, "You bitch!" The savage blow knocked her sideways and tipped over the chair, sending her to the floor. Beth screamed as she saw her niece being attacked.

The fusillade from the fireplace was over now, but guns were going off outside. As she huddled on the floor, Melinda felt a grin of triumph tugging at her mouth. She had warned whoever it was outside that he was walking into a trap.

Now it was up to him.

As he was running up the hill, Longarm caught a glimpse of the guard at the rear of the house ducking around the corner toward the front. Well, he thought, he had wanted a distraction. He was getting it even earlier than he had hoped for.

He reached the top of the slope and headed for the back door of the house. Barely pausing long enough to lift his leg, he drove the heel of his boot against the lock and slammed the door open. He went into the house with the shotgun leveled.

Guns were still crashing toward the front. Seeing no movement, Longarm headed in that direction. He tried to remember the layout of the house, but he hadn't really seen any of it except the parlor. He came out there a moment later, shouldering through a doorway.

Instantly, his eyes took in the scene. He saw Beth and Melinda Crawford tied in chairs facing each other near the big stone fireplace. Melinda's chair had overturned so that she lay on the floor. A few feet away from them was one of the outlaws. The man had been facing the fireplace, but he whirled around at the sound of Longarm's entrance. The holster on his hip was empty, Longarm saw, but the outlaw reached desperately behind his back, no doubt going for a hideout gun.

Longarm couldn't use the scattergun; the women were too close, and some of the buckshot might hit them as it spread out. He let go of the Greener with his right hand and sent it flashing toward the Colt in the cross-draw rig, but the outlaw had a split-second lead on him. The man was able to yank the gun from behind his belt in the small of his back. The small pocket pistol cracked spitefully, and the slug it spat whipped past Longarm's ear.

By that time, though, Longarm's Colt was in his hand,

and the revolver bucked against his palm as he triggered it. The .44-caliber bullet drove into the outlaw's chest and flung him back toward the fireplace. He fell, his left arm in the leaping flames, and the sickly-sweet stench of burning human flesh began to fill the room.

The fact that the outlaw didn't jerk his arm out of the fire told Longarm that he was dead. The lawman's shot must have found his heart.

Longarm twisted toward the front door as he spotted movement there from the corner of his eye. Holding the shotgun in his left hand, he fired one barrel. The charge of buckshot hit the door and blew a hole out of it, sending whoever was trying to get in diving back the other way with a frantic yelp. Shots blasted just outside the door, and bullets whined as they ricocheted around the room. All Longarm could do was hope that they missed Beth and Melinda—and him.

He knelt behind a heavy divan and leveled the barrels of the greener at the door. One barrel was still loaded, and if the outlaws outside knew that, they would think twice about charging blindly through the door. Longarm was counting on their caution to give him a momentary respite.

As the gunfire died away outside, Longarm called softly without turning his head away from the door, "Are you ladies all right?"

"I'm not hit," replied Beth. She added anxiously, "What about you, Melinda?"

"I'm fine," she said. "None of the shots hit me."

"I'm all right, too," came a man's voice, surprising Longarm.

He glanced over just long enough to see Nick Larson, the lawyer from Greybull, huddled on the floor on the far side of the fireplace. Larson's hands were tied behind his back, just like Beth and Melinda. Longarm hadn't noticed him before because the lawyer had been lying behind a heavy ottoman.

He didn't know what Larson was doing here, but it didn't really matter. The lawyer was obviously a prisoner, too. Longarm said, "Can you get over here, Larson?"

"I . . . I can try."

Nick got onto his knees and began scooting toward Longarm. Keeping his right hand on the shotgun, Longarm used his left to fish out his folding knife. He opened it with his teeth. "Turn around," he said when Larson reached him.

It took only a few seconds for the keen blade to sever the cords around Larson's wrists. Larson gasped as they fell away. He had been tied so tightly that his hands were probably numb.

"Rub your hands together," Longarm told him. "As soon as you've got enough feeling back, take the knife and cut the women loose."

"All r-right," said Larson. He rubbed and shook his hands for a moment, then clumsily picked up the knife and started crawling toward Beth and Melinda, keeping low in case more bullets started flying.

An ominous silence had fallen. Longarm still had no idea what had provoked the shooting outside. It was obvious, though, that the remaining outlaws were in no hurry to charge the house.

At least two of Stennett's men were dead. That left him with four men, at the most. But five to one odds were still pretty bad, Longarm reflected. He wasn't sure how much help he could count on from the three former prisoners.

Suddenly, a shout came from outside. "Hey!" The deep voice belonged to Bull Stennett, Longarm figured. "Who the hell's in there?"

Longarm didn't see any point in concealing his identity. "Deputy Marshal Custis Long!" he bellowed back. "Better throw down your guns and surrender while you got the chance, Stennett! My posse'll be here any minute!"

That was a bluff, of course, but Stennett couldn't know

that. If Longarm had gotten out of Salem Valley, then the rest of the posse could have, too.

From somewhere down the hill, Stennett laughed. "You're the one who'd better give it up, lawman!" he called. "Otherwise I'm goin' to blow the head off this young fella I've got here with me!"

Longarm's jaw clenched. What in blazes was Stennett talking about . . . ?

Then, suddenly, with sinking spirits, Longarm thought he knew. A second later, his guess was confirmed when a nervous voice called, "I think he means it, Marshal!"

Harley Kincaid.

23

Longarm's teeth ground together in anger and frustration. What the devil was Harley doing here? The youngster should have been on his way back from Greybull by now with a sawbones for the old-timer called Buck and a posse to help Longarm round up the Stennett gang.

Instead, Harley was a prisoner of the gang. Did that mean help wasn't coming? Longarm was afraid that was probably the case. Harley must have started toward town, only to change his mind and decide to ride back to his father's ranch. Longarm knew that Harley had been upset about the possibility of outlaws taking over the MK, but he hadn't expected the youngster to disobey his orders.

"Hold on, Stennett!" he shouted. "Don't let that trigger finger of yours get itchy!"

"It already is, lawman! Come out of there with your hands up, or I'll shoot this kid!"

Longarm knew Stennett meant every word of the threat. He muttered, "Damn!" and came to his feet.

Nick Larson had managed to cut the two women loose. Beth Crawford began, "Marshal, you can't—"

Longarm turned his head and said sharply, "Take your niece and get out of here, ma'am. Larson, you go with 'em and see that they're safe."

157

"But . . ."

"Do it," snapped Longarm.

Reluctantly, Larson and the two women started toward the rear of the house. As they left the parlor, Longarm moved closer to the front door, which stood partially open.

"I'm throwing out my guns!" Longarm called to Stennett. "Hold your fire!"

He tossed the Greener through the open door onto the porch, then followed it with the Henry rifle and his six-gun. The little derringer that was welded to a chain attached to his watch was in his pocket, and he took it out and slid it down the side of his boot. The outlaws would probably search him, but they might not find the derringer there.

A moment later, he heard footsteps on the porch. The door was kicked open, and a burly figure came through it quickly, gun leveled. Longarm stood still, his hands raised to shoulder height. As he studied the muscular, hard-faced outlaw, his gut told him he was looking at Bull Stennett himself.

"So you're the star packer who's been doggin' my trail," Stennett said with a snarl.

"It's my job to bring in thieves and murderers," Longarm said calmly. He knew he might have only seconds to live. Stennett might gun him down like another man would swat a fly.

Stennett surprised him by lowering the barrel of his gun slightly. "Bring the kid in," Stennett ordered over his shoulder. A couple of seconds later, another outlaw shoved Harley Kincaid through the door.

Longarm saw right away that the left sleeve of Harley's coat was bloodstained. The youngster had been wounded while trading shots with the outlaws. But the injury didn't look too bad, and Harley didn't seem to be wounded anywhere else. His face was pale and frightened, but his voice was fairly strong as he said, "I'm sorry, Mr. Long. I reckon I've fouled everything up."

"Don't worry about it, Harley," Longarm told him. "You did what you thought was best."

"But I should've gone to Greybull to fetch that posse like you told me!" Harley cried miserably. He lifted his hands and covered his face as if he were ashamed. "Now there's nobody to help us!"

But even as he spoke, Harley parted the fingers on his right hand so that his right eye was visible, and the eyelid went up and down in a deliberate wink that only Longarm could see. What the hell? Was Harley trying to tell him that help really *was* on the way?

Longarm didn't let his confusion show on his face. He maintained his stony expression as he said, "Don't worry, kid. We'll get out of this somehow."

Stennett laughed harshly. "I don't know how you figure that, Long. You and this worthless son of a bitch are both unarmed, and nobody knows you're here."

Longarm didn't say anything. Stennett seemed to have forgotten about Beth, Melinda, and Larson. They'd had time by now to slip out the back of the house and reach the trees. If they could escape into the foothills and find some help . . .

The door at the rear of the parlor opened, and Melinda Crawford let out a little cry as one of the outlaws shoved her into the room. "You were right, Bull," the owlhoot said. "They tried to get out the back while this lawman stalled you."

For the second time in the past quarter of an hour, Longarm's heart sank. A couple of the gang herded Beth and Larson into the room after Melinda. Stennett had thought and acted quickly enough to thwart their escape, and now he had five hostages.

The only hope remaining to Longarm was a slender one. Harley had winked at him about something. He

159

hoped he could stay alive long enough to find out what it was.

The man Longarm had killed with the shotgun was called Dawson. The one in the barn had been Travis. The four men he had left were Leon, McClatchie, Mills, and Carlson. Longarm heard those names as Stennett ordered one of the remaining bandits to go dig some graves for them.

Stennett didn't seem to be in any hurry to kill anybody else, and Longarm was grateful for that much. Stennett had believed Harley when the young man said that there was no posse coming from Greybull. He thought he had all the time in the world to continue looting the ranch and terrorizing his prisoners.

Longarm had been tied hand and foot and pushed down onto the sofa. Beth and Melinda were bound back into the same chairs they had occupied earlier. The outlaws settled for tying the wrists of Harley Kincaid and Nick Larson. Stennett stood guard over them himself while another outlaw cooked dinner and the remaining three desperadoes patrolled around the house, just in case anybody else showed up tonight.

One of the bandits had a rag tied tightly around his jaw, which seemed to be busted, and Longarm wondered what had happened to him. The man kept casting fearful glances toward Stennett whenever he was in the room with the boss outlaw. Longarm wondered if Stennett himself had inflicted the injury.

He wanted to ask Harley why the youngster had come back to the MK and what that wink had meant, but he couldn't with Stennett hovering close by. So he had to be patient and wait for a chance.

Melinda said, "We're sorry we got caught again, Marshal Long. When we went out the back door, one of those outlaws was waiting for us."

"Ain't your fault, ma'am," Longarm said with a reassuring smile. "Just bad luck, that's all."

Misfortune had dogged his steps all along the way on this case, he reflected. Maybe Billy Vail had been so mad at him for stealing away the attention of that pretty female reporter that he'd put a hoodoo of some sort on his chief deputy. Longarm grinned to himself at the thought. Billy Vail was as down-to-earth an hombre as ever trod the plains. The idea of him putting a curse on somebody was downright ridiculous.

No, it was just bad luck, thought Longarm, especially today. The last really good thing that had happened to him had been early that morning, when Melinda had done her little striptease show for him. . . .

Thinking about that, remembering the nude beauty he had been privileged to witness for a brief moment in the cabin, he looked at Melinda now and felt a wave of sympathy. Her honey-blond hair was in disarray, her clothes were disheveled, and she was pale and frightened looking. He vowed to himself once again that he would find a way to get the young woman and her aunt out of this mess.

The bushy-bearded outlaw called McClatchie, who had been given the cooking chores, carried in a bowl of beans and some biscuits for Stennett. Longarm asked, "What about the rest of us? Don't we get to eat?"

Stennett thought it over for a second, then inclined his head toward the prisoners and said, "Bring them some food, too."

McClatchie nodded. "Sure, Bull." He started out of the parlor, then said, "Can I gag that old fart who's tied up out there in the cook shack? He keeps cussin' me."

"Yeah, go ahead," agreed Stennett.

When McClatchie had left, Harley Kincaid asked, "Was he talking about Horse Collar?"

"If that's the name of the old man who cooked around here, that's right," Stennett said around a mouthful of beans. "He ain't dead."

Harley looked relieved.

"Yet," added Stennett.

Harley started to flare up, but Longarm caught the young man's eye and shook his head. Annoying Stennett wouldn't gain them anything right now.

McClatchie came back with a pot of beans and a spoon. He fed each of the prisoners in turn while Stennett stood nearby with a gun drawn, making sure none of them tried any tricks. Longarm hadn't eaten since breakfast, so he was grateful for the food. The others seemed to be, too.

When the meal—such as it was—was finished, Stennett asked mockingly, "Now I reckon you want some brandy and cigars."

"Sounds good, old son," drawled Longarm. "I'd rather have a shot of Maryland rye, though. Why don't you look around and see if there's a bottle of Tom Moore in the house?"

Stennett's lips pulled back from his teeth. He stepped closer and backhanded Longarm, a savage blow that jerked the lawman's head to the side and rattled his teeth. "You're lucky I don't kill you right now!" he growled.

Longarm worked his jaw around for a second, then licked away the trickle of blood he felt coming from the corner of his mouth. He didn't like it, but he managed to force out a hoarse, "Sorry."

The apology mollified Stennett. "That's better. You damned well ought to be grateful for your life." He looked around at the other captives. "All of you. I could snuff out your lights just like *that*." He snapped his fingers.

"And yet you keep us alive," said Beth. "Why?"

Stennett shrugged. "A fella never knows when he'll need some bargaining chips. I don't expect any other lawmen to show up here before I'm ready to leave, but if they do, they'll think twice about chargin' in with guns blazin' while I have hostages in here."

That made sense, thought Longarm. Stennett was an outlaw, but he wasn't a fool. When he was ready to leave the MK, though, he would have no further need for the hostages.

That was when the killing would start.

After a few minutes, Stennett began pacing around the room. "This is a hell of a note," he said. "A nice hideout like this, and there ain't nothin' to do." His eyes fell on the women, and he grinned lecherously. "Well, almost nothin'. Maybe it's time I got better acquainted with you ladies."

Longarm spoke up quickly. "Are you a gambler, Stennett?" he asked.

Stennett looked at him with a frown and repeated, "A gambler?"

"Thought you might be a man who likes a good game of cards."

The boss outlaw snorted. "I like a hand or two of poker as well as the next man, but you ain't got any stakes, star packer."

"Well, that ain't strictly true," said Longarm. "I could bet my life."

Stennett laughed and held out his hand, palm up, then slowly curled it into a fist. "I already got that right here. And I can take it any time I want."

Longarm shrugged. "If you don't want to play, that's fine."

"Wait a minute," Stennett said sharply, frowning again. "Just what sort of bet are you talking about, Long?"

"Like I said, my life." Longarm paused, then added, "Against yours."

"What the hell?"

"One hand of poker," continued Longarm. "If you win, you go ahead and shoot me. Four hostages are just as good as five, especially when two of 'em are women."

"And if you win?" asked Stennett.

Longarm looked him intently in the eyes. "You give me my gun back, and you and me face each other, old son. You still got a chance to gun me down. All you got to do is outdraw me."

Stennett gave a harsh bark of laughter. "What kind of

fool's bet is that? I already got you right where I want you. Why in blazes would I give you a chance to shoot me?"

Longarm grinned. "You said you liked to gamble."

He was the one gambling, he realized. He didn't know if he could goad Stennett into the bet, and even if he won, he didn't know if he could shade the outlaw when it came to a showdown.

But he couldn't sit by and do nothing while the women were molested, either. He had to stall Stennett some way, in hopes that his hunch was right and help was really on the way.

Stennett regarded him moodily for a long moment. Longarm scarcely dared to breathe while the outlaw made up his mind. Then, abruptly, Stennett nodded.

"One hand of poker," he said, "but the stakes ain't goin' to be exactly like you said, Long."

"What did you have in mind?" Longarm asked.

"If you lose . . ." Stennett drew his gun and pointed it at an ashen-faced Harley Kincaid. "I don't go ahead and shoot you. I shoot *him*."

Longarm didn't even look at Harley as he said, "It's a bet."

24

Longarm could feel the gazes of the other prisoners on him, but he didn't look at them. He knew what he would see there: fear in Harley's eyes, mingled dread and relief in those of Beth and Melinda, confusion in Nick Larson's. Actually, they probably all wondered what the hell he was doing.

Welcome to the club, thought Longarm dryly. He wasn't sure himself why he had challenged Stennett, other than to distract him from the women and buy a little more time.

Those reasons would just have to be good enough.

And so would his poker-playing, since Harley's life was riding on it.

Stennett called in Leon, a tall, hatchet-faced outlaw, and told him, "Cut the marshal loose, then step back and keep your gun on him."

"What are you goin' to do, Bull?" asked Leon.

Stennett grinned. "The law dog feels like playin' a little game, so I'm goin' to oblige him."

Leon looked dubious, but he pulled a knife from his belt and sawed through the bonds around Longarm's wrists. Then he stepped back quickly and drew his gun as Stennett had ordered.

Slowly, Longarm brought his arms in front of him. He rubbed his hands together to get some feeling back in them, taking his time about that, too. He massaged his wrists, flexed his fingers, rolled his wrists around on their joints.

"Stop stalling," snapped Stennett. "Are we playin' cards or not?"

"We're playing," Longarm assured him. "I figure you want a fair game, though. Who's going to deal? I can, if you want."

Stennett glowered suspiciously at him. "How do I know you ain't a cardsharp?"

"You reckon I moonlight from my marshal's job as a tinhorn?" Longarm gibed. Although, truth be told, he could handle a deck of pasteboards just about as well as a lot of professional gamblers. He knew all their little tricks, too.

"All right, you can deal," Stennett agreed. He looked around the room. "Where's a deck of cards?"

Longarm glanced at Harley, who swallowed hard and said, "In the desk in my pa's study."

"Thanks," Longarm said quietly. He hoped Harley understood about the way he'd put his life on the line.

Stennett went into the study and came back a minute later with a deck of cards. He slapped them down on a table and then said to Longarm, "All right. Deal."

Longarm looked down at his feet, which were still bound together. "How am I supposed to get over there?" he asked.

"Hop," Stennett told him with an ugly grin.

Longarm grunted, then carefully stood up from the sofa. Balancing himself precariously with his arms, he started hopping across the room toward the table, his boot heels thumping against the floor each time he landed. He felt the derringer in his right boot where it had gone unnoticed. It would take him only a second to stoop, pull the derringer from his boot, and put a slug in the middle of Stennett's grinning face.

But if he did that, Leon would just shoot him in the back the next second, and the other prisoners wouldn't be any better off than they were before.

He would wait and see how the game played out, Longarm decided.

He finally reached the table and leaned on it for a moment before picking up the cards. He riffled through the deck to see that all the cards were there, then started shuffling. Stennett stood on the opposite side of the table, his hand resting on the butt of his gun.

When Longarm was satisfied that the cards had been shuffled sufficiently, he placed the deck in the center of the table and said, "Cut."

Stennett cut the deck about in the middle, swapped the cards, then put the deck down. Longarm picked it up and said, "Five-card draw?"

"You're the dealer," said Stennett.

Longarm dealt the cards. When both hands were lying face down on the table, he put the deck down and picked up the cards he had given himself. It had been a straight deal, nothing off the bottom or out of the middle of the deck, nothing palmed up his sleeve.

And despite that, the hand was a pretty good one anyway: a pair of jacks, a nine, a ten, and a queen. He could fill the straight two ways, or he could throw away the nine and the ten and try for two pair or three of a kind. He glanced at Stennett but couldn't read any expression on the outlaw's face as Stennett studied his cards.

After a moment, Stennett looked up. "With the stakes what they are, there's no need for betting and calling."

With a nod, Longarm agreed. "I'd say the ante's about as high as it can get."

"I'll take three cards, then," Stennett said as he separated three of the pasteboards in his hand and tossed them aside.

Longarm dealt the three. Still no change in Stennett's expression as he picked them up and looked at them. The outlaw had a good poker face, all right. Longarm debated whether to go for the straight.

"Dealer takes one," Longarm said casually—a lot more casually than he felt—as he made his decision and threw away one of the jacks.

"Mighty confident," commented Stennett.

"No reason not to be," said Longarm as he dealt a single card face down in front of him and then set the deck aside before he picked it up.

He was willing it to be an eight or a king, but his luck ran true—and bad. A lady stared regally up at him from the new card. A second queen. He had improved his original hand from a pair of jacks to a pair of queens, but that was all. He looked up at his opponent.

"Well," said Stennett, "are we goin' to stand here and stare at each other all night, or are we goin' to lay down our cards?"

"I reckon we'll lay down our cards," said Longarm.

He would have to make that try for the derringer after all, he thought, otherwise Stennett would murder Harley in cold blood. The little .41 carried two bullets. He would have to put one of them into Stennett, then turn and get Leon with the other one. Of course, Leon would get him, too, but that couldn't be helped. . . .

Longarm used his left hand to place his cards face up on the table. Stennett did likewise. Utter silence filled the room, so much so that when a piece of wood popped in the fireplace, it sounded as loud as a gunshot and made everyone jump except Longarm and Stennett.

"Well, what do you know?" Stennett said softly.

"Yeah," husked Longarm, his mouth and throat dry. "What do you know?"

Stennett looked down at his cards. The eight and the king that Longarm had wanted were there, along with another eight, a six, and a three.

168

"A damned lousy pair of queens," said Stennett. "Beaten by a pair of queens."

Longarm didn't know yet whether to be relieved or not, didn't know whether Stennett would abide by the terms of the bet. He said, "The ladies were good to me."

"Leon," Stennett said, "cut the ropes on the lawman's legs and give him a gun."

Leon practically yelped in surprise. "Give him a gun!" he repeated. "Bull, what are you doin'?"

"That was the bet," Stennett said harshly. "If Long won, he'd have his chance against me."

"But . . . but what if he beats you to the draw?"

"Then I reckon you'll be the new leader of the gang, since Tom hasn't come back from visiting that redheaded whore of his. You can do whatever you want with these folks."

Leon looked confused and worried, but he followed Stennett's orders, bending over to cut the ropes around Longarm's ankles. Again, Longarm went through the routine of regaining full sensation in his extremities. As he did so, he glanced over at the other prisoners. Harley looked relieved, naturally, but still worried. The others watched anxiously, too.

Leon had an extra six-gun tucked behind his belt. Longarm recognized it as his own Colt, and just as he had hoped, the outlaw took it out and handed it to him. If Stennett noticed that Longarm had his own gun back, he didn't say anything about it. The familiar grips of the revolver felt mighty good against Longarm's hand as he wrapped his fingers around them. He checked the cylinder, saw that all the chambers were full except the one the hammer was resting on, and slid the weapon into its holster.

A part of him was waiting for some treacherous move on the part of Stennett. His brain couldn't fully accept the idea that a ruthless killer such as the outlaw leader would face him in a fair fight. But he would play this out for as long as he could, thought Longarm. If he downed Stennett, he would take his chances with Leon and the other outlaws.

Stennett moved into an open area in the parlor and faced Longarm. He opened and closed his right hand several times as it hovered over the butt of his gun. "I'm ready when you are, Long," he said harshly.

"Never be in a hurry to die, old son," Longarm said. Without looking around, he made a mental note of Leon's position. If he could get both of the outlaws, that would leave only the three outside to deal with, and one of them was hurt. Suddenly, things were looking a lot better. Longarm's desperate ploy might actually work.

First things first, he reminded himself. He still had to kill Bull Stennett.

He swung around slowly until he was facing Stennett. The same eerie silence that had hung over the room during the hand of poker had the place in its grip once more. No one except the two men facing each other seemed to be breathing.

"Anytime you're ready, Long," Stennett said in a half whisper.

But before either man's hand could dart toward a gun, the outlaw called McClatchie burst through the door at the rear of the room and yelled, "Bull!"

Stennett reacted instinctively. He grabbed for the gun on his hip as he pivoted smoothly around. The Colt's barrel came up and lined itself on McClatchie's chest, and Stennett's finger tightened on the trigger.

The bearded outlaw yelped in surprise and fear and threw his hands up. "Don't shoot, Bull!" he cried out. "It's me!"

At the same instant, Longarm's hand flashed across his body and palmed out his Colt. He wheeled toward Leon, but the hatchet-faced gunman was already moving. He swung his weapon like a club, smashing the barrel against Longarm's head. Longarm reeled and almost went down.

Leon grabbed his gun wrist and forced the Colt toward the floor.

Slow! You're too damned slow! a voice screamed in the back of Longarm's brain. The long, violent day and the injury he had suffered were taking their toll on him, and his actions weren't as swift as they normally were. Leon slashed at him again with the gun, but this time Longarm was able to avoid the blow. He grappled with the outlaw for a second.

Then something hard ground into his spine and Stennett grated, "Drop it, Long, or I'll blow you in half!"

Longarm froze. To his disgust, Leon yanked the gun out of his hand. He was unarmed again, except for the hidden derringer.

Longarm looked around. Somehow, Stennett had stopped himself from pulling the trigger on McClatchie, though the bearded outlaw was sweating and pale from the close brush he'd had with death.

"McClatchie says he heard a bunch of riders coming this way," Stennett said. "Got any idea who they are, Long?"

Longarm shook his throbbing head. "Not a clue."

Stennett pointed the gun at him and snapped, "You're a damned liar!"

Harley Kincaid burst out, "It's a posse from Greybull! The jig's up, Stennett. You might as well surrender."

Longarm grimaced. He wished Harley had kept Stennett in the dark and off-balance for as long as possible. But what was done was done.

"A posse?" the boss outlaw repeated.

"That's right," Harley went on triumphantly. "I was on my way to Greybull to fetch help myself, but then I ran into a rider who was headed that same direction. He said he'd carry the message for me, so I came back here to help Marshal Long." The young man looked sheepishly at Longarm. "Sorry it didn't work out that way, Marshal."

"Don't worry about it, old son," Longarm told him. "At

least now I know you didn't just completely ignore what I told you to do."

"I would've gone on to Greybull, but I thought I could be more help here."

"Shut up!" barked Stennett. "I don't care who did what. All I know is, if you think you're safe now, boy, you got it all wrong." He eared back the hammer of the gun in his hand. "We may all go down fightin', but you'll be dead first!"

And he swung the barrel of the gun toward Beth Crawford.

25

Longarm tensed his muscles, ready to throw himself toward Stennett. He was too far away, though, and feared that he wouldn't be able to reach the outlaw in time to stop him from shooting Beth.

With a yell, Nick Larson lunged up out of the chair where he had been sitting. He flung himself between Stennett and Beth just as Stennett pulled the trigger. The bullet slammed into Nick and spun him off his feet.

Harley came out of his chair, too, lowering a shoulder and diving into Leon from behind. Leon's gun went off, but the slug thudded harmlessly into the ceiling as the outlaw's arm was knocked upward by the impact.

Leon caught his balance before he could fall and slung Harley away from him, but by that time, Longarm had dipped his hand into his boot and come up with the derringer. As Leon's gun barrel dipped toward Harley's head, Longarm fired one barrel of the little weapon. The .41-caliber slug bored into Leon's skull just above his left ear. Leon staggered a step to his right, then went down like a puppet with cut strings. He was dead when he hit the floor.

Longarm swung toward Stennett, hoping the shot that had killed Leon would distract Stennett away from the women. Sure enough, Stennett was aiming at Longarm now. The bandit leader's revolver roared, sending a slug whipping past Longarm's ear. Longarm squeezed off his second and final shot from the derringer, but Stennett twisted aside in time to avoid the bullet. Unarmed for the moment, Longarm dove toward Leon's fallen body and reached for the gun the dead outlaw had dropped. Another of Stennett's bullets chewed splinters from the floorboards next to Longarm.

Even as his fingers wrapped around the butt of the gun for which he was reaching, Longarm rolled desperately to the side. Stennett fired and missed again. Longarm snapped a shot at him with Leon's gun, but Stennett threw himself headlong behind the heavy sofa where Longarm had been sitting earlier.

Longarm glanced at Beth and Melinda. They seemed to be all right, but they were both pale with fear. Longarm didn't blame them. Enough lead was flying around in this room to scare anybody. He rolled on underneath a table, then reached up with his leg and kicked the bottom of it so that it overturned, falling between him and Stennett. Bullets might punch through the table, but it was better than no cover at all.

Breathing hard, Longarm stretched out on his belly and crawled to the edge of the table. He risked a quick glance around it but didn't see Stennett anywhere. Nor could he hear the outlaw moving. From here, he couldn't see Beth and Melinda, either, but he heard Melinda just fine as she shouted, "Look out, Marshal! To your left!"

Longarm twisted in that direction, bringing the gun up as Stennett rushed him. Bullets from the boss outlaw's gun whined past Longarm's head and smacked into the table. Longarm triggered the weapon in his hand, but as he did so, his eyesight suddenly blurred and doubled, no doubt from the bullet crease on his head and all the frantic activity of this violent day.

There were two Bull Stennetts now, and Longarm

wasn't sure which one to shoot at. Both of them were roaring curses and firing at him.

He'd just have to kill both of them, Longarm decided, and as if he were shooting at two separate opponents, he squeezed off a round, smoothly shifted his aim to the other Bull Stennett, and fired again. Both Stennetts stopped, swayed for a second, then stumbled forward, struggling to bring up their guns.

Longarm squeezed the trigger again and heard the metallic click of the gun's hammer falling on an empty chamber. He was out of bullets, and the sound echoed like a death knell. Both Stennetts grinned ugly grins, and despite the blood welling from identical holes in their chests, their guns steadied for one final shot.

The booming explosion that echoed through the room in the next second didn't come from Stennett's gun. Instead, as Longarm's vision finally cleared again so that the twin figures merged back into the one that it really was, Stennett was driven backward by the impact of a heavy slug that caught him in the chest. His gun thudded to the floor, and the outlaw leader himself followed it a split second later.

"Buck!"

Longarm heard Beth Crawford cry out the old-timer's name, so he wasn't too surprised when he pushed himself up off the floor and saw Buck standing just inside the rear door of the parlor. Smoke curled from the barrel of the old Walker Colt in his hand. That was probably the same gun Buck had used when his potshot kissed Longarm's skull several nights earlier, but today the old man hadn't missed with it.

Longarm saw his own gun lying on the floor nearby. He tossed Leon's empty revolver aside and scooped up the Colt. He came to his feet and walked rather unsteadily over to where Stennett lay. The outlaw was on his back, his arms outflung to the sides. His eyes were open, but they were staring sightlessly up at the ceiling with no sign of life in them. Bull Stennett was dead.

"Buck, where on earth did you come from?" asked Melinda.

Longarm was curious about that, too, since the last time he had seen the old man, Buck was so badly wounded that he shouldn't have been able to even roll over, let alone get out of bed, make his way to the MK, and help Longarm gun down Stennett.

At the moment, however, there were still three outlaws outside to worry about. Longarm was surprised McClatchie, Mills, and Carlson hadn't come rushing in when all the shooting broke out. Maybe they were waiting to bushwhack the posse from Greybull. . . .

That thought reminded Longarm to ask Buck, "Did you see a posse outside, old-timer?"

Buck snorted. He was still holding the Walker Colt, but it was down alongside his leg now. "Dadgum it, you keep talkin' about how old I am," he complained. "You ain't no spring chicken yourself, you know!"

Longarm wasn't going to argue that point. Right now, he felt about a hundred years old, and that was the truth. He just said, "The posse?"

Buck shook his head. "There ain't no posse. Leastways, none that I seen."

Harley had struggled to his feet with his hands still tied behind his back. He said, "But . . . that outlaw came running in and said he heard them coming. . . ."

Buck waved his free hand and cackled. "If there's one thing I'm good at, it's makin' a racket."

Longarm frowned. He didn't see how one old man could make enough noise to sound like an entire posse, but he wasn't going to question some good fortune for a change. He moved over beside Nick Larson, who was breathing harshly. Longarm knelt and rolled the lawyer over. Nick yelped in pain.

"You'll be all right, old son," Longarm told him after

a quick examination of his wound. "Looks like that bullet tore a chunk out of your upper arm, but it appears to have missed the bone. Just lay still and try not to bleed too much."

"The . . . the women?" Nick gasped out.

"They're all right. We all are." Longarm stood, nodded toward Leon's body, and said to Buck, "Get that fella's knife and cut the ladies loose. Harley, too."

Buck sniffed. "Mighty fast to give orders now that I done saved your bacon, ain't you?"

"I'm going to take a look around outside," Longarm said, ignoring Buck's comment.

Carefully, with his gun held ready for action, he stepped to the front door and opened it, then eased outside. The night was still and quiet now. Of course, that didn't mean anything. The remaining outlaws could be forted up anywhere out here, their fingers on the trigger just waiting to blaze away at anything that moved.

But after spending half an hour exploring around the ranch house, the barns, and the corrals, Longarm had to come to the conclusion that McClatchie, Mills, and Carlson were gone. Three horses were missing from the bunch the outlaws had ridden here. Thinking that a posse was about to swoop down on them and hearing a sudden outbreak of gunfire from inside the house, the three men had done the sensible thing. They had taken off for the tall and uncut.

Stennett had been the driving force of the gang. Without him to lead them, the three survivors wouldn't be much of a threat. They would be behind bars within six months, Longarm guessed. Either that, or gunned down in some botched holdup.

As soon as he got a chance, he would send a wire to Billy Vail and have the chief marshal alert all the local authorities in Wyoming about the three outlaws, Longarm decided. Right now, though, he had other matters to tend to.

He went back inside and reported that McClatchie, Mills, and Carlson were gone. He found that the women had bandaged Nick Larson's wound and had him stretched out on the sofa, where they were fussing over him and apparently making Harley Kincaid a little jealous. Melinda was holding a cup of water so that Nick could drink, and Harley was watching with a slight frown on his face.

"First thing in the morning, Harley," said Longarm, "you're going to ride to Greybull. And you're actually going to get there this time."

"But I told you I sent the message, Marshal," Harley protested.

"I reckon you did, but something could've happened to that rider you ran into. His horse could've stepped into a hole and broke a leg, or he could've got throwed off, or he might have run into some other bad luck. It won't hurt for you to go and make sure we've got some help on the way. Your pa and the rest of the hands are still trapped up there in Salem Valley, remember."

Beth Crawford faced Longarm squarely and said, "If you had taken our advice, Marshal, and stayed away from Salem Valley, none of this would have happened."

Longarm shrugged. "Maybe so, but then Stennett and his bunch would still be loose, and as soon as the weather got better, they'd have gone right back to robbing and killing."

"Well, I suppose you're right about that," Beth said reluctantly. "You can understand, though, why a part of me wishes you'd never come here."

"Yes, ma'am," Longarm agreed. "But I had a job to do."

Beth looked at him for a moment, then smiled faintly and nodded. She went over to help Melinda see to Nick Larson.

Longarm turned his attention to Buck, who still had an unfriendly glower on his whiskery face. "I didn't expect to see you again so soon," the lawman commented.

Buck shrugged his bony shoulders. "I got to feelin' a mite better, so I figgered I'd come over here and see if I could lend a hand." He looked at Beth and Melinda, and for the first time Longarm heard affection creep into the old man's voice. "I was mighty worried about them two. My job's to watch over 'em, and I didn't do it too good."

"You got here in time to help save them," Longarm pointed out, "when most hombres who are shot up as bad as you are would be lucky to live."

Again Buck shrugged. "I heal faster'n most folks."

To tell the truth, the old man was moving around as if he hadn't been wounded at all. Buck had put on a flannel shirt, and Longarm suddenly wished he could take a look underneath the garment. He had a crazy notion that those bullet holes in Buck's scrawny carcass might not be there anymore. Longarm remembered reading in the past that witches didn't always have to be female. There were male witches, too, and after a moment, he was even able to recollect what they were called.

Warlocks.

But that really *was* a crazy notion, Longarm told himself as he took a deep breath. He gave a soft laugh and muttered under his breath, "I really have been hit in the head too much lately."

"What'd you say?" Buck demanded.

"Nothing, old-timer, nothing."

"Old-timer? There you go again, blast it. . . ."

26

Longarm was so exhausted that he slept deeply and dreamlessly in a bed in one of the spare bedrooms in the MK ranch house. He was so tired that he dozed off as soon as his head hit the pillow, and it wouldn't have surprised him if he'd slept for a week.

But he woke up quickly enough when he realized that an armful of warm, nude female flesh was snuggling up against him.

He opened his eyes and looked into the blue eyes of Melinda Crawford at a distance of about three inches. She smiled down at him and said cheerfully, "Good morning."

Longarm's arms went instinctively around her. "Good morning your ownself," he replied. One of his hands moved down underneath the quilts that covered them to caress the smooth, silky curve of her rump. "Does your aunt know that you done crawled naked into my bed like a shameless hussy?"

"No, but I don't care whether she knows or not. She's been trying to shelter me from real life for a long time now. Too long. After the last couple of days, I think it's time she let me grow up some."

With that, Melinda lowered her head and her mouth found Longarm's. Her kiss was hot and hungry, and when her tongue darted against his lips, Longarm opened them so that she could thrust it into his mouth.

His shaft had been hard when he awoke, and by now it was so stiff between them that it throbbed achingly. Melinda ground her bare stomach against the long, thick pole of male flesh. There was a certain small awkwardness to her movements that told Longarm she didn't have a lot of experience in lovemaking, but she more than made up for it in enthusiasm.

He broke the kiss and warned her, "Better simmer down a mite or we're going to be sticky."

"I want to be sticky inside from you, Marshal!"

"Well, if we're going to do this," said Longarm, "maybe you'd better call me Custis."

"All right, Custis," she said brightly. "What would you like to do first?"

"I reckon that's sort of up to you. . . ."

"I know what I want to try, then," said Melinda. She pushed the covers back, and even though the air in the room was a little chilly, Longarm didn't mind. His blood was thundering through his veins powerfully enough to keep him plenty warm as Melinda turned herself around and lowered her head over his groin. She wrapped both of her hands around his manhood and began licking the crown of it.

Longarm groaned, tempted to just lie back and revel in the pleasure of what she was doing to him. He liked to be fair about such things, though, so he took hold of her hips and shifted her so that she was straddling his head with her soft thighs. As he looked up, he had a nice close view of the puffy pink lips of her femininity, topped off by the pertly puckered opening in the valley of her rump.

As Melinda kept licking and nibbling on the head of his shaft, Longarm used his fingers to peel open the tight slit between her legs. He wasn't sure if she was a virgin or not, but if any lucky young gent had been in here, it hadn't been very often. He ran his tongue along the lips, then slipped it inside her.

Melinda gasped and clamped her thighs against Longarm's ears as what he was doing to her sent spasms of delight through her body. He hung onto her hips to keep her from jerking around too much as he continued to probe her femaleness with his tongue. He thought about sliding a finger up her ass, but he decided that would be too much sensation for someone as inexperienced as her. He didn't want her passing out on him.

She still had hold of his shaft, but as the waves of pleasure cascaded through her, she forgot to pay any attention to it. Longarm didn't mind. He figured she'd get back to it eventually.

Before she could, though, the door of the room suddenly swung open, and Beth Crawford stepped inside, wrapped in a silk robe. She stopped short, her eyes widening. With the covers on the bed thrown back like they were, she had a good view of her niece with her open, panting mouth hovering just over Longarm's rampant manhood. Longarm heard the door opening and twisted his head to the side so that he could peer past Melinda's smooth flank. He saw Beth standing there, an expression of shock frozen on her face.

Then, slowly, Beth took a deep breath and closed the door behind her. "Melinda!" she said sharply. "What are you doing?"

From the way Melinda jumped, Longarm didn't think she had even been aware of her aunt's entrance. She looked up and started stammering, "Aunt B-Beth! I . . . I didn't . . . We j-just . . ."

"I can see for myself what you and the marshal are doing," Beth said sternly. "It's very improper."

"I . . . I'm sorry, Aunt Beth. . . ."

"You should be." Beth untied the belt around her waist and slipped the robe off her shoulders. Her bare breasts came into view as the robe opened, and then she shrugged it off completely so that it fell to the floor in a silken puddle around her feet. "The marshal is giving you so much enjoyment, and you're neglecting him."

Longarm tried not to grin smugly as Beth walked toward the bed. He had been worried for the first few seconds after she came into the room, but then he had seen the fires burning in her eyes.

"Sit up," Beth told Melinda as she climbed onto the foot of the bed and positioned herself between Longarm's legs. "Marshal, you go right ahead with what you were doing. I want you to watch, though, Beth, so you'll know what to do the next time you find yourself in such a position."

With that, her head swooped down and her mouth opened to engulf Longarm's shaft. She took in at least half of it and began sucking.

"Oh," Melinda said, as if understanding had just dawned on her. Then she said, "Oh!" again, much more forcefully this time, as Longarm stuck his tongue inside her again.

This wasn't the first time in his life Longarm had found himself in bed with two gals at the same time. He remembered a pair of sisters over in Idaho who had damned near killed him one night with their competitive urges.

There was no competition between Beth and Melinda, though. They worked together. There were so many smooth, bare arms and legs intertwined on the bed that Longarm sort of lost track who was doing what to whom, or some such. He knew that at one point Beth and Melinda were taking turns giving him one hell of a French lesson, giggling amongst themselves as they handed his pole back and forth. After watching that for a few minutes, he was surprised that his climax didn't erupt all over their faces. Somehow, though, he maintained control.

Finally, it was time for Melinda to experience the rest of what he had to give her. She straddled his hips and lowered herself toward him. Beth knelt right behind her and reached down to grasp Longarm's shaft. She aimed it so that Melinda came down right on it and held it until the younger woman was completely filled. Melinda threw her head back, closed her eyes, and gasped with joy. Her hips began to pump as she rode Longarm.

Beth embraced her from behind, cupping Melinda's breasts in her hands. She rested her head on Melinda's shoulder and smiled down at Longarm, then began licking Melinda's neck.

With all of that going on, Longarm knew he wasn't going to be able to last very long. But Melinda was galloping to her climax, too, so she didn't seem disappointed a few minutes later when it overtook her. She cried out and ground her pelvis against Longarm's. He thrust up hard, burying his shaft as deeply within her as he could. His seed began to explode inside her. Spasm after spasm shook both of them as he emptied himself into her in a hot, wet flood.

Melinda's eyes rolled up in her head, and she sagged to the side, practically falling off of him. Longarm's back had been arched up off the bed, but he fell back, too.

Beth smiled down at him. "I want some of that, too," she said, "but I'll wait my turn."

That was good, thought Longarm, otherwise he'd be heading back to Denver in a pine box.

But he had to chuckle as he wondered just how Henry would write up the report on *that*.

All in all, it was a couple of weeks before Longarm started home. He'd gone to Greybull and sent a wire to Billy Vail advising the chief marshal that Bull Stennett, Tom Morgan, and most of the rest of the Stennett gang were dead. In the message, Longarm just happened to mention that he'd suffered a head wound in the course of tracking down the gang, and Vail had generously wired back for Longarm to take as much time as he needed to recuperate.

The fact that a blizzard roared down out of Montana a

few days later made Longarm more than happy to spend some time at the MK. Beth and Melinda were there, too, having accepted the ranch's hospitality while their own cabin was being rebuilt.

After a couple of times, though, the two women didn't slip into his bed anymore. Melinda was too busy enjoying the attentions of Harley Kincaid and Nick Larson, who quickly developed a spirited rivalry over her. Nick's wounded arm was healing well. Longarm watched the courtship dance among the young people with amusement. He just hoped that their affection for Melinda wouldn't drive a wedge between the two old friends. Whoever wooed her successfully was going to be one lucky gent, that was certain.

Beth Crawford, to Longarm's surprise, began to take an interest in Martin Kincaid. The crusty, middle-aged rancher had been rescued, along with his crew, from Salem Valley after several days when a group of volunteers from Greybull finally managed to dig through the cave-in blocking the hidden tunnel. Kincaid had been surprised, and not too happy at first, to discover that the Crawford women were staying on his ranch. Now that the secret of Salem Valley had been uncovered, though, there was no more talk of witches and curses, and Beth assured Kincaid that she had no designs on his ranch. So he decided to file a claim on the land.

It wouldn't have surprised Longarm too much to learn, though, sometime in the future, that the two ranches had been joined together. And let no man put them asunder, he added to himself.

When the weather cleared, a warm spell took hold. The deep snow that had clogged the roads and the passes began to melt, at least enough so that Longarm knew he would be able to make it to Laramie and then on to Denver. Before he left, though, he rode over to the Circle Moon with Beth and Melinda to check on things. Martin Kincaid gruffly volunteered to go along, too, and of course neither Harley nor Nick, who was spending more time on the ranch than he did at his law office in Greybull, could allow the other one to spend that much time alone with Melinda.

Over the objections of the women, Buck had been staying at the Crawford ranch to supervise the construction of the new cabin. He seemed to be fully recovered from his wounds. He was nowhere around, though, when the group rode in. Several of the hands from the MK were working on the cabin. Beth, Melinda, Kincaid, Harley, and Nick walked over to watch them.

Longarm grinned as he stood there holding the reins of his horse. He was going to miss these folks. They had been enemies for a while, and Longarm was glad they had put that behind them, even though it had taken a day and a night of blood and death to do so.

He looked over at the corral and saw the old gray-and-white cat sitting on one of the rails. Longarm meandered in that direction. The cat watched him suspiciously but didn't run off this time. Longarm reached out and scratched the animal behind its ears.

The cat began to purr—grudgingly, it seemed to Longarm—then stood up and stretched, balancing easily on the log rail. Longarm frowned as he saw two small bald spots on the cat's back, scarred places where something had injured the animal and the fur hadn't grown back.

If the cat had been human, thought Longarm, those scars would be in about the same places as old Buck had been shot by those outlaws. . . .

He wondered if there were matching scars on the cat's chest.

He might have actually lifted the animal to check, if at that moment the cat hadn't turned and bit him on the hand. Longarm jerked his fingers back. "Damn it—"

The cat glared up at him. Longarm glared right back at it for a moment, then said, "You're right. I reckon it's time I went back to Denver before I go as crazy as everybody else around here."

He would have sworn the cat nodded.

With a shake of his head, Longarm turned away and swung up into the saddle. Some sort of argument was going on among the group over by the cabin, but it didn't sound serious to him. It sounded like the type of good-natured squabbling that went on between people who cared about each other.

Grinning, Longarm pulled the horse around and heeled it into a trot that carried him to the south.

Watch for

LONGARM ON THE BORDER

280th novel in the exciting LONGARM series
from Jove

Coming in March!